The Great Unexpected

Also by
SHARON CREECH

The Boy on the Porch
The Unfinished Angel

The Great Unexpected

Sharon Creech

Andersen Press • London

This paperback edition first published in 2013 by
Andersen Press Limited
20 Vauxhall Bridge Road
London SW1V 2SA
www.andersenpress.co.uk

2 4 6 8 10 9 7 5 3 1

First published in 2012 in the United States of America by Joanna Cotler
Books, an imprint of HarperCollins Publishers.

British Library Cataloguing in Publication Data available.

ISBN 978 1 84939 659 2

Printed and bound in the UK by CPI Group (UK) Ltd., Croydon, CR0 4YY

for
Pearl and Nico
and
for you, reader

So much world all at once...
—Wislawa Syzmborska

Overheard Conversations

Father and four-year-old son:

Father: Did you brush your teeth?
Son: Yes.
Father: Really?
Son: Yes.
Father: Tell me the truth.
Son: What is 'truth'?

Mother and five-year-old daughter:

Daughter: I'm going to be a dolphin.
Mother: Is that so?
Daughter: Yes. I will live in the ocean.
Mother: For real?
Daughter: What is 'real'?

Contents

Prologue

My name is Naomi Deane and I grew up in Blackbird Tree, in the home of my guardians, Joe and Nula. Among the tales that Joe often told was that of a poor man who, while gambling, lost his house but won a donkey.

'A donkey?' the poor man wailed. 'What do I want with a donkey? I cannot even feed a donkey.'

'No matter,' replied the donkey. 'Reach into my left ear.'

The poor man, though shocked that the donkey could talk, nonetheless reached into the donkey's ear and pulled out a sack of feed.

'Well, now,' the poor man said. 'That's a mighty handy ear. I wish it had food for *me* as well.'

'Reach into my right ear,' the donkey said.

And so the poor man reached into the donkey's right ear and pulled out a loaf of bread, a pot of butter and a meat pie.

Joe went on like this, spinning out the tale, with the poor man pulling all sorts of things out of the donkey's ears: a stool, a pillow, a blanket and, finally, a sack of gold.

I loved this story, but I always listened uneasily, fearing that something bad would be pulled from the donkey's ears. Even after I'd heard the tale many times, always the same, I still worried that the poor man might reach in and pull out a snapping turtle or an alligator or something equally unpleasant and unexpected.

Sensing my fear, Joe would say, 'It's only a story, Naomi, only a story.' He suggested that I say to myself, '*I'm not in the story, I'm not in the story*' – a refrain I could repeat so that I would feel less anxious.

And so each time the poor man would reach into the donkey's ears, I would tell myself, I'm not in the story, I'm not in the story, but it didn't help because a story was only interesting if I *was* in the story.

CHAPTER 1

A Body Falls from a Tree

I f you have never had a body fall out of a tree and knock you over, let me tell you what a surprising thing that is. I have had nuts fall out of a tree and conk my head. Leaves have fallen on me, and twigs, and a branch during a storm. Bird slop, of course, everyone gets that. But a body? That is not your usual thing dropping out of a tree.

It was a boy, close about my age, maybe twelve. Shaggy hair the colour of dry dirt. Brown trousers. Blue T-shirt. Bare feet. Dead.

Didn't recognize him. My first thought was, *Is this my fault? I bet this is my fault.* Nula once said I had a knack for being around when trouble happened. She had not been around other kids much, though, and maybe did not know that *most* kids had a knack for being around when trouble happened.

All I really wanted to do that hot day was go on down to

the creek and hunt for clay in the cool, cool water. I was wondering if maybe I could deal with the body later, when the body said, 'Am I dead?'

I looked at the body's head. Its eyes were closed.

'If you can talk, I guess you're not dead.'

The body said, 'When I open my eyes, how will I know if I'm dead or alive?'

'Well, now, you'll see me, you'll see the meadow, you'll see the tree you fell out of, so I guess you'll know you're alive.'

'But how will I know if I'm here or if I'm at Rooks Orchard?'

'I don't know anything about any rook or any orchard, so I can pretty much guarantee that you are here and not there. Why don't you open your eyes and have a look around?'

And so the body opened his eyes and slowly sat up and looked all around – at the green meadow, at the cows in the distance, at the tree out of which he had fallen and at me, and then he yelled, 'Oh, *no!*' and fell back on the ground and his eyes closed and he was dead again.

CHAPTER 2

Lizzie

No sooner had the body lain back down than I heard the warbling voice of Lizzie Scatterding. Lizzie often felt it necessary to sing – in a high, trembly, warbly opera voice – when she was outdoors.

'Oh, lar-de-dar, the sky so blue' – definitely Lizzie – 'the fields so green, oh lar-de-dar—'

Lizzie was my friend, and usually I was glad to see her, but I was not sure how she was going to handle seeing the body at my feet. Sometimes Lizzie could be a little dramatic.

'Oh, lar-de-dar – Naomi! Is that you?' Lizzie stopped in the middle of the path and crossed her hands over her chest as if to keep her fragile heart steady. 'Naomi!' She ran towards me, her frizzy mane flopping here and there.

'Ack! Naomi, what is *that*? Is that a person?' She inched her way around to stand behind me so that I was her shield. 'Who is it? Where'd it come from? Is it *dead*?' She clutched my shoulders. 'You didn't *kill* it, did you?'

'It fell out of this here tree. I thought it was dead, but then it spoke, and now it's gone off again.'

I kneeled beside the body and put my hand on its chest.

'Is it breathing?' Lizzie asked. 'Take its pulse.'

I held the body's wrist. 'I can feel something gurgling in there.'

'Oh, my! Then it's alive. Have you ever seen it before? What did it say when it spoke – before it went off again?'

'Something about a rook's orchard, or maybe a crook's orchard.'

Lizzie's foot nudged the body's foot. 'Maybe it was in an orchard place and a crook tried to kill it and so he hid in this tree and then when you came along—'

'Maybe we should stop calling it an *it*.'

Lizzie studied the body's face. 'Never saw it before, did you?'

'Nope.'

'Look in its pockets, Naomi. See if it has something with its name on it.'

'I'm not looking in any boy's pockets, dead or alive. You look.'

Just then the body grunted. Lizzie skittered sideways like a crab.

'Good gracious! I swear to bats! It's alive!' Her hands were protecting her fragile heart again. 'Naomi, the poor *thing*. What if his internal organs are hurt? What if he is bleeding to death and we don't even know it? Naomi, you must get help.'

The body spoke. 'Am I here – ?'

Lizzie squealed. 'It has a voice!'

Its eyes were still closed. 'Am I here – or am I there?'

I touched his hand. 'You're here.'

'How will I know that?'

'Well, ding it, you are *here*. If you weren't here, you wouldn't be hearing me, would you? You'd be somewhere else. But you're not somewhere else, *you are here!*'

'Naomi, you don't have to be so harsh. It's a poor body lying there maybe bleeding to death and it just wants to know if it is here.'

'Fine. Then you take over, Doctor Lizzie.'

'I *will*.' Lizzie carefully placed herself beside the body, folding her legs daintily beneath her. 'Now,' she cooed in the softest of tones, 'everything will be just fine. We need to find out who you are and if you are injured in your internal organs.'

The body was silent.

Lizzie inched a little closer. 'Boy, can you tell me your name?'

Silence.

'Boy, do you have family around here?'

Silence.

'Naomi, do you have a cool cloth?'

'No, Lizzie, I do not happen to have a cool cloth on my person.'

'I feel we should put a cool cloth on this poor injured boy's forehead.'

'I don't have a cool cloth.'

Lizzie sighed a deep, meaningful sigh. 'Oh, dear, oh, dear.' She lightly touched her fingers to the boy's head. Then she leaned closer and blew on his forehead.

'Whatever are you doing, Lizzie?'

'I am cooling the poor boy, Naomi. I am bringing comfort until such time as he can rouse himself.'

'What if he can't ever rouse himself? What if he dies for good?'

Lizzie tapped the boy's shoulder. 'Please do try your best to rouse yourself and tell us your name.'

Silence.

'I am pleading with you, boy.'

Silence.

'Naomi, you will have to get help. I will stay here with the poor, injured boy. Please go. Please hurry.'

But before I could move, the boy spoke again. 'Don't take the gold.'

'Naomi, he spoke! He told us not to take the gold!'

'I've got ears, Lizzie. I heard him.' I tapped his arm. 'What gold?'

Silence.

I scanned the area. No gold in sight. I asked louder: 'WHAT GOLD?'

'Naomi, please don't shout at the poor, injured boy.'

The boy opened his eyes.

'Naomi, he opened his eyes.'

'For heaven's sake, Lizzie, I'm not blind.'

'My name is Finn.'

'Naomi, he said his name! He said his name! His name is Finn!'

'There isn't any gold,' he said.

'Naomi, he said—'

'I know, I know what he said. There isn't any gold. There isn't any silver, either. There aren't any emeralds or rubies or diamonds—'

'He didn't say any of that, Naomi. He only said about the gold.'

'No gold,' the boy repeated.

'See?' Lizzie said. 'No gold.'

CHAPTER 3

Across the Ocean: Revenge

Mrs Kavanagh

While Naomi and Lizzie were learning the name of the body that fell from a tree, across the ocean in a stately manor on the southeastern coast of Ireland, the elderly Mrs Kavanagh paused as she wrote on a piece of fine parchment. She placed the pen to one side and tapped a finger on the desk.

'There. Enough for now.' She smiled a wistful smile. ''Twill be a fine, fine revenge.'

Her companion, Miss Pilpenny, recapped the pen. 'Yes, Sybil, a fine and clever revenge.'

'Shall we have a murder tonight?'

'Indeed, Sybil. Splendid notion.'

'And then perhaps a little jam and bread.'

'Indeed. That plum jam from the Master's orchard?'

Old Mrs Kavanagh laughed, a sudden girlish burst that was followed by prolonged wheezing.

Miss Pilpenny rubbed the old lady's back until the wheezing subsided. 'There, there. You can rest now.'

CHAPTER 4

The Body Speaks

The body named Finn asked if we had any sweets on us.

'Candy?' I said.

'Yes. Can-dee,' he said, as if he had never said the word before.

Then he asked if we had any can-dee drink.

'Candy drink?' Lizzie said. 'Whatever do you mean, Finn boy?'

By this time, Finn had sat up and commenced to scratching himself: his head, his neck, his belly, his ankles. 'You call it, wait, you call it – soda pop. You got any of that?'

You could take one look at me and Lizzie and see that neither one of us was carrying anything whatsoever, so where would we be stashing soda pop?

'No soda pop,' I said.

Apparently Lizzie thought I was too abrupt. She smiled at Finn and put her hands together under her chin. 'I think this boy needs some refreshment, Naomi. I think this boy is hungry and thirsty.'

'I think this boy is old enough to say what he wants, Lizzie. I think this boy is not invisible.'

Lizzie ignored me. 'Finn boy, are you entirely sure you are not bleeding from your internal organs? Because if you are, you should not move, and we should send Naomi for help. But if you are not bleeding from your internal organs, then perhaps we should escort you home, if you would be so kind as to tell us where that might be, Finn boy.'

'No. No help,' Finn said, leaping to his feet.

'Oh, my,' Lizzie said. 'Are you entirely sure you should be upright?'

'I'm fine, fine.' Finn rotated his head and his hands. He lifted one foot and then the other. 'I'll be going now.' Finn turned and started off across the meadow.

'But wait,' Lizzie called. 'Wait, wait, Finn boy!' She ran up behind him. 'Won't you let us escort you home? What if you become faint along the way? What if—'

'I can make it fine.'

Lizzie was protecting her fragile heart again. 'But, Finn boy, at least tell us where you live. We've never seen you in these here parts before.'

Finn looked to the left and right and then to the sky above. 'I'm staying up the hill a piece.'

'Up that hill?' I said. 'Black Dog Night Hill?'

'That's what you call it? That's where I'm headed.'

'But nobody lives up there, nobody except the—' I looked at Lizzie. She looked at me. 'Nobody except the dim Dimmens clan.'

Lizzie batted at me with her hand. 'Shh.'

Finn looked right in my eyes, calm as could be, and said, 'That's where I'm staying, up at the dim Dimmenses' place.' With that, he continued on his way with only the slightest limp.

'Look what you've gone and done, Naomi.'

'What? What'd I do?'

'You called them the "dim" Dimmenses. That's so rude.'

'That's what everybody calls them. That's what you call them.'

'But not to their – their – house guest.'

"House guest'? Since when did you start calling company 'house guests'?'

'Oh, Naomi. That poor, injured boy. That poor, poor Finn boy.'

CHAPTER 5

The Moon

Lizzie joined me at the creek, where we dug clay for an hour or two. We found a good grey clump of it, smooth as could be, beneath the top gravelly layer. Perfect for making bowls and such. Lizzie felt obliged to talk.

'Naomi, I can't help worrying over that poor, injured Finn boy. What if he has fallen on the path and no one finds him for days or weeks and he dies all pitiful and alone and then goes rotten and the raccoons eat him up? I can hardly bear the thought. Where do you think he came from, Naomi? Why do you think he's staying with the dim Dimmenses up on Black Dog Night Hill? Do you think he's kin to them? That would be the most awful shame.'

Joe, my guardian and a man of few words, once said about Lizzie, 'That girl could talk the ears off a cornfield.'

'Naomi, do you think I should ask the Cupwrights to investigate?'

'No, Lizzie, I do not.'

Mr and Mrs Cupwright were Lizzie's foster parents. They were strict beyond strict and believed in minding their own business. Mr Cupwright's favourite comment was, 'Don't know nothin'. Ain't none of my business.'

If you asked Mr Cupwright about his brother Ned, Mr Cupwright would say, 'Don't know nothin'. Ain't none of my business.'

If you asked Mr Cupwright if his other brother was out of jail yet, he would say, 'Don't know nothin'. Ain't none of my business.'

Lizzie had been with the Cupwrights for two years, ever since her parents died up in Ravensworth, one right after the other. She said her mother died of 'diseases' and her father died of heartbreak. Her only aunt was 'a little funny in her head,' and her only uncle was homeless in Michigan. The Cupwrights told Lizzie they might adopt her, but that was two years ago and they hadn't mentioned it since. Lizzie was hopeful, though.

'Oh, Naomi,' she said, 'I know they would adopt me if they could get everything in their lives to run more smoothly, and what with the barn falling over and the cow stuck in the pond and the electric wires catching fire, they have a lot of other things to worry about right now. I will have to bide my time.'

Sometimes Lizzie would say, 'I need to go and stand on the moon awhile,' and she would look up into the sky and close her eyes and breathe deeply, and then a few minutes later, she'd open her eyes and smile and say, 'There. Much better.'

Lizzie said that if you imagined you were standing on the moon, looking down on the earth, you wouldn't be able to see the itty-bitty people racing around worrying; you wouldn't see the barn falling in or the cow stuck in the pond; you wouldn't see the mean Granger kids squirting mustard on your white dress. You would see the most beautiful blue oceans and green lands, and the whole earth would look like a giant blue-and-green marble floating in the sky. Your worries would seem so small, maybe invisible.

The first time I tried standing on the moon, what I saw in my mind was a million billion people, every one of them with problems, all running here and there and screaming for help. It was a scary trip to the moon.

When we were there in the riverbed digging clay, Lizzie closed her eyes and went to stand on the moon, and when she came back to earth, she said, 'There. Much better.'

I was going to have to practise that moon-standing more often because it was remarkable the change in Lizzie when she came back from the moon. She had been wading in the water, troubled about 'that poor Finn boy' from her toes to her frizzy hair, but after standing on the moon, she had the most peaceful look on her face.

'Naomi! I know exactly what to do!'

'And what's that?'

'You and me – together we will go and find Finn!'

'I can't. I need to get home.'

'You silly, I don't mean today. I mean *tomorrow*.'

CHAPTER 6

Across the Ocean: The Solicitor

MRS KAVANAGH

I t was late when the solicitor arrived at Mrs Kavanagh's. It was long past the entertaining murder and the jam and tea. Mrs Kavanagh's companion, Miss Pilpenny, answered the bell.

'I do apologize,' Mr Dingle said. He was a tall, slim man, immaculately dressed in tweeds fashionable decades earlier. The faint smell of mothballs trailed after him. 'Mrs Kavanagh did say it was permissible to come after the theatre.'

Miss Pilpenny nodded. 'And sure it is fine and not all that late for the pair of us, now, is it?'

Mrs Kavanagh was seated in her usual place beside the fire. The ancient fireplace let as much smoke into the room as up the chimney, but this did not seem to bother Mrs Kavanagh.

'Charles,' she said to Mr Dingle. 'How good of you to come.'

'My pleasure entirely.' Mr Dingle glanced around the sitting room. With a wink, he said, 'I see you've taken down all the Master's portraits.'

Mrs Kavanagh smoothed the blanket on her lap. 'The fool. The bombastic, cruel fool.'

'The room looks so much brighter now.'

'The whole house is so much brighter now,' Mrs Kavanagh said. 'The whole garden. The orchard. The whole town!'

'That one man could cast such darkness over people – simply intolerable.'

'And yet – and yet – we tolerated, didn't we? You tolerate or you go hungry. But enough of that, Charles. Here are the papers. I'd like you to read them through and see if all is in order.'

Miss Pilpenny tapped at the door. 'Would you like some sherry, Mr Dingle?'

Mr Dingle brightened. 'Yes, indeed. Yes, thank you.'

'Sybil?'

Mrs Kavanagh put her fingers to her lips. 'Mmm, yes, lovely.'

After the sherry had been sipped and the papers had been studied, Mr Dingle leaned towards Mrs Kavanagh. 'Absolutely splendid, Sybil. You see, things do right themselves in the end, don't they?'

'But do you see any obstacles here?'

'I will have to investigate a few matters—'

'I've appreciated your investigations over the years. This time, I'd like for you, personally, to go to the States and pave the way.'

'Absolutely. You read my mind.'

'I wish I could join you, but these old legs, alas—' She tapped her knees with her cane. 'These old legs and these old bones will not last much longer.'

'Sybil—'

'Now, now, let's not pretend. I am ancient as the hills; I am ready to go now that my revenge is in place.'

Miss Pilpenny, reentering the room on those last words, said, 'And a fine, fine revenge it is.'

Mr Dingle rose from his chair. 'Indeed.'

CHAPTER 7

Nula and Joe

'I can see you've been to the creek, girl, what with the clay on your cheeks and in your hair and all about your clothes, isn't that right, Naomi?'

She wasn't mad. This was the way Nula talked. When I was little, we'd play Mean Gran and Poor Little Girl. Nula would put on a mean voice and say, 'For the love of sausage, girl, you are not going to leave this house until you clean every inch of it.'

And I would reply in my most feeble voice, 'Oh, no, please. Please let poor little me go out in the sunshine.'

Nula would whack a wooden spoon on the counter and say, 'Don't pull those tears on me, you little worthless lump of dust. Wash the floors. Wash the windows. Wash the dishes. Wash the bedding…'

'Poor, poor pitiful me. I am a poor child all alone in this world.'

'Quit your moanin', lass, and get to work!'

And so I would rush around, madly waving rags over everything, pretending to clean.

So now when I came back from digging clay in the riverbed with Lizzie, Nula said, 'No gruel for you tonight unless you wash all those clothes and clean up your shoes!'

Nula and her husband, Joe, took me in when I was three years old. I don't think they intended to keep me, but I guess they never got around to finding another place for me. They said I could call them Gran and Grandpa, and sometimes I did, but more often I simply called them Nula and Joe. I didn't realize I wasn't related to them until I went to school.

If you looked at Joe, you wouldn't guess he had a sense of humour. He was a short, wiry, bowlegged man who walked with a rocking gait. His face usually sported grey stubble with which he could 'beard' mischievous children. Tufts of grey hair stuck out of his head. He didn't smile. He always looked as if he'd just heard bad news. Joe didn't talk much, but he'd occasionally drop a line or two that caught you by surprise and made you laugh. He didn't laugh back, though. Instead, he would act as if he couldn't understand what was so funny. You had to watch his eyes and his mouth. If his lips were closed and moving about as if he were chewing on them from the inside, and if his eyes looked sparkly, then he was teasing you.

Nula was in many ways Joe's opposite. She was taller than Joe by a good ten centimetres, plump and soft-looking, with hair the palest, palest, faded red mixed with white and piled loosely on the top of her head. Nula's real name was Fionnuala,

pronounced *fin-NOO-luh*, but most people called her simply
Nula (*noo-luh*). She was proud of her Irish roots and her Irish
name, but unless you were born and bred in Blackbird Tree and
your parents were born and bred in Blackbird Tree, you were
and always would be a foreigner, and you'd best keep your
'strange ways' to yourself.

When Joe came in from the fields and we three sat down to
dinner, I told them about the body falling out of the tree.

'Now, which tree would that be?' Joe asked.

I said it was the one with the green leaves on it.

Nula said, 'Ah, lass, I know exactly which one you mean.
The one with the branches, right?'

Joe's lips were moving about.

'That's the one, Nula. So the body falls out of the tree and
knocks me over and I think it's dead. It wasn't moving or
anything.' I told them about Lizzie coming along and blowing
on his forehead and all, and how he didn't want any help and
his name was Finn.

'Finn?' Nula said. 'Finn? Not a name you hear much around
here, though I knew a few Finns back in my time, that's for
certain. There was Finn O'Tanoran and Finn Murphy and Finn
O'Connor – a charmer, that one. And oh, Finn McCoul – you'd
best stay away from him. Finn, eh? And where did he come from
and where is he now?'

I said I didn't know where he came from, but he was headed
up Black Dog Night Hill.

'He wouldn't be living up at the Dimmenses' place, now,
would he?' Nula asked. 'Finn? Are you sure he said *Finn*?'

Then Nula wanted to know how old the boy was and what he looked like and if his clothes were clean or dirty and if his hair was tended to or shaggy and was he barefoot or did he wear shoes and if he wore shoes, were they proper-fitting shoes?

That night, after I went to bed, Nula leaned into my room to say good night. Then she said, 'Finn? Are you sure it was Finn?'

'Pretty sure.'

'Mmm-mm. I knew some Finns in my day, I did.'

CHAPTER 8

Families

Two years ago, we had a teacher who didn't last long. She arrived full of sparkle and new clothes and manicured fingernails. On the very first day, she gave us an assignment. We were to write about our families.

'Which ones?' someone asked.

'Why, the ones you live with, of course. Your *families*. You know, your mother, your father, your sisters, your brothers.' She smiled at us as if she were thinking, *The poor, ignorant dears, they do not even know what the word* family *means*.

So the next day, we straggled in with our precious essays about our ragtag families. She made us read them aloud. Well, the first five people, that is.

Angie lived with a foster family with eight children and four donkeys and seven cats and three snakes. Her real parents were still in jail.

Lizzie lived with her foster parents, who were definitely going to be her adoptive parents, and they had no other children because her foster mother got headaches. Her real mother had had headaches, too, but that was from 'diseases that made her die'; her father died 'of the maximum grief'.

Carl lived with his uncle, who lost both his legs in a car crash, and so Carl had to do all the cooking and cleaning and grocery shopping and it wasn't too bad except when his uncle got ahold of the liquor.

Delano said he wasn't allowed to write about his family while they were under investigation.

And then there was me. I told about my mother giving birth to me and on the second day of my life, she looked at me and said, 'Gosh, I feel peculiar,' and then she dropped me on her stomach and died of a blood splot that went where it wasn't supposed to go. I started to tell about how my father died of an infection, but the teacher stopped me.

'Oh, my,' she said. 'Oh, dear.' She turned her back to us and rummaged in her bag for a tissue and blew her nose, and then still with her back to us, she said, 'Excuse me for a minute, please,' and she left the room.

'What?' I said, when everyone turned to look at me. 'Is it my fault? Again?'

The next morning I told Nula that I couldn't go to school because I had turned into a fairy.

'Really, now? And what does that have to do with school?'

'Fairies don't go to school, you ought to know that. And I

won't be wearing shoes any more because fairies don't wear shoes. And I might have to move soon . . . to a *flower*.'

The 'families' teacher lasted only three months. She told Mrs Tebop over at the general store that we were 'simply too tragic'.

We didn't think we were tragic. We thought we were normal. All any of us wanted was for somebody to care about us, and if we couldn't have that, then at least somebody who wouldn't be too mean and who would feed us from time to time. I suppose the only thing I wanted beyond that was that it wouldn't be my fault. What 'it' was, I couldn't say. But 'it' was usually bad and always unexpected.

CHAPTER 9

Black Dog Night Hill

Lizzie and I stood at the base of Black Dog Night Hill, not a place I wanted to be.

'Lar-de-dar,' Lizzie warbled, 'it looks completely fine.' She was referring to the path that led up the hill. 'Those are probably only rumours about the black dog and the yellow eyes and the skeletons. There is probably not an ounce of truth to them, and I really do not believe that the Dimmenses keep trespassers in chains. How silly is that? How – how – ridiculous. Right, Naomi?'

'Uh-huh.'

'How many of them do you think live up there now, Naomi?'

'Dimmens people? Nula says it's a whole clan. Maybe fifty.'

'Fifty? But isn't there just one cabin?'

'Last I heard there was only the one.'

'Then, truly, Naomi, fifty people cannot live in one cabin.'

The day was cloudy and cool, with enough breeze to keep the mosquitoes away. Poison ivy trailed along one side of the path; nettles clumped along the other side. A garter snake slithered from the ivy to the nettles.

'Ooh!' Lizzie said. 'Eww. Surprised me, that's all. Eww. We'll go a little ways and see what we see, OK?'

'Not going.'

'Ten paces, let's just go ten or thirty paces.' Lizzie chattered as she walked. Reluctantly, I followed. 'I do not understand why people are so hard on the poor Dimmens family,' she said. 'I think it is a downright shame that the children have to be home-schooled now because they don't get along with anyone. If those parents would teach them some manners, then maybe they would get along with people and could come to school like normal people.'

'I thought they were home-schooled because it was too far to trek back and forth to school every day.'

'Oh. Wait! Listen. Hear that? A *dog*?'

She said *dog* the way most people might say *skunk* or *bobcat*.

'Hear that, Naomi? Was that a dog? What if it's the black dog, Naomi? The one with the yellow eyes and the dripping blood, the one that jumps to your throat, the one that—'

I was already up the nearest tree.

We listened. Something was coming through the brush.

Lizzie was as pale as a potato. 'We're going to *die*.' She scampered up the tree after me.

We heard a rifle shot. Then another. A small red fox dashed

across the trail and dived into the bushes on the other side. A boy with a rifle, not in any hurry, appeared on the path.

It was Finn.

'Don't you dare shoot that fox,' I called. 'Don't you dare.'

Finn swivelled towards me and my tree perch. 'Who said anything about shooting it? What're you two doing up there?'

'Nothin.'

'Seems a funny spot for two girls to be doing nothin.'

'Naomi is scared of dogs,' Lizzie said.

'Lizzie!'

'Well, she is.'

'I don't see any dogs, but that explains her up the tree,' Finn said. 'What about *you*?'

'I was keeping Naomi company,' Lizzie said, jumping to the ground.

I could've punched her.

'Aren't you coming down?' Finn asked.

'I'm fine where I am.'

'She's *afraid* of *dogs*,' Lizzie said.

Finn looked up at me. 'You? Didn't I hear that you gave Bo Dimmens a black eye?'

'Who'd you hear that from?'

'Bo himself.'

'He was asking for it. He kept tripping me, and I got mighty tired of falling face-first in the dirt.'

Finn nodded. 'And didn't I hear tell that you knocked out some boy's tooth?'

'That tooth was already loose.'

'And didn't I hear you had an imaginary pet, a dinosaur—'

'You sure hear a lot,' I said.

Lizzie felt obliged to chime in. 'Her dinosaur was toothless. It drank flesh shakes. *Flesh shakes.*'

'Is that right?' Finn said. He stared up at me. 'Seems to me that a girl as tough as you oughtn't be afraid of a dog.'

Lizzie said, 'Her daddy got eaten by a dog.'

'What?'

'Lizzie, you shut your mouth.'

Lizzie shrugged. 'Well, he did. And look at her arm. Dog did that. Nearly chewed it off. That's why it's so shrivelled up.'

'You nut head, Lizzie.'

Finn's mouth was hanging open. He looked from me to Lizzie and back again.

I still wasn't coming down out of the tree. I made myself comfortable up there.

'Finn boy,' Lizzie said, 'are there really fifty people living up there at the Dimmenses' place? I mean, I know it's not any of my business, but people do talk and they're saying that at least fifty people live up there, and I say, "How can that possibly be true, what with the Dimmenses' place being so little and all?" Mmm?'

'I don't think there are fifty people up there. Not that I've seen, anyhow. There might be fifty *dogs*—'

'What?' I said, feeling as if I might lose my breakfast right then and there. '*Fifty?*'

'I didn't exactly go around counting them.'

Now, here is an odd thing. While I was stuck up in that tree with an icy fear of those dogs, I took a sudden liking to that Finn boy. I can't hardly explain it. He was standing there with the sun coming down on his light brown hair, and his face was rosy gold with splashes of freckles across his cheeks, and he had a smudge of dirt right there under his right eye and he didn't look like anyone I'd ever met. He seemed to fit so easily in his body, unlike the other, clumsy boys around. His mouth was curved up a little at the corners so that he always looked as if he were smiling or about to smile.

Lizzie said, 'Finn *boy*—'

'Why don't you call me Finn? That's my name. Not Finn boy.'

'OK. Finn, is there really an evil black dog that stalks this hill and terrorizes trespassers?'

'I haven't heard about that yet. I haven't been here long.'

'Where'd you come from? When did you get here?' I asked. I couldn't help it. When I wanted to know something, I wanted to know it *now*.

'Naomi!' Lizzie said. 'Naomi Deane, that's a little forward. Maybe the boy doesn't want to tell us where he came from or when he got here.'

'Lizzie, maybe the boy can decide for himself.'

'It's a long story,' Finn said. 'It's complicated.'

CHAPTER 10

Across the Ocean: Dogs Sleep

Mrs Kavanagh

Mrs Kavanagh was seated in her wheelchair beneath a pear tree. Across her lap lay a blue cashmere shawl and at her feet curled two sleek hound dogs, white with tawny patches. They were foxhounds, sisters from the same litter, distinct with their long, slender legs and gentle, narrow faces.

Mrs Kavanagh eased her foot out of its slipper and lightly traced the nearest dog's foreleg with it. 'There, there, Sadie,' she said. 'No one will split you and Maddie.'

Overhead, two young squirrels chased each other through the branches, loosening leaves and pieces of bark. Mrs Kavanagh watched as these pieces drifted to the ground. She was reminded of another day, long ago, in the small village of Duffayn, when her younger sister had come running across the meadow, calling, 'Sybil, Sybil!'

Now, another figure was crossing the meadow. Mrs Kavanagh squinted. It was Pilpenny.

'Sybil, Sybil—'

Mrs Kavanagh heard the edge in Pilpenny's voice.

'Sybil, you've a visitor.'

CHAPTER 11

The Crooked Bridge

When I asked Finn where he was from, he said, 'You know where the Crooked Bridge is?' He was sitting on the ground, Lizzie was standing nearby, and I was still up in the tree.

'What kind of crooked bridge?' Lizzie said. 'You mean an old wobbly bridge? We've got lots of those around.'

'I mean *the* Crooked Bridge. That's the name of it: Crooked Bridge.'

'Never heard of it,' I said.

So Finn went on to describe the bridge. It was wooden, and it crossed a narrow river. Its shape was zigzag. He drew a diagram in the dirt.

'Looks like a silly way to build a bridge,' I said.

Finn said it was built that way so evil spirits chasing you would miss the turns and zing off the ends and into the water.

'Think of *that*,' Lizzie said. 'I love it to pieces and pieces! What a great idea!'

'*If* you believe in evil spirits,' I said, 'and if you believe that they'd miss the turns and zing off the ends.'

'Doesn't sound like the girl in the tree thinks the Crooked Bridge is real,' Finn said.

I didn't like how suddenly I was on the outside of this conversation. 'The girl in the tree has a name,' I said. 'Naomi. And I didn't say I didn't think the Crooked Bridge was real. I just don't think the evil spirits part is real.'

'You don't believe in evil spirits?'

Lizzie hugged herself as if she were cold. 'Oh, *I* do, *I* do believe in them. Maybe Naomi doesn't, but I do.'

'So is that where you live?' I said. 'Near this Crooked Bridge?'

'No.'

'Then why were you telling us about it?'

'Thought it was interesting, that's all.' He stretched and yawned. 'So what's this place called again?'

'Which place?' Lizzie said. 'This here place where you're sitting or this here place roundabouts?'

'Uh—'

'Blackbird Tree,' I said. 'That's what this here town is called. Don't you even know where you are?'

'What's near here?'

'Nothing,' I said.

'Well, shoot, Naomi, of course we are near *something*. Sure, some people hereabouts call this place Lost Tree – that's a little joke, see? Do you know they didn't get electricity here until about a hundred years after everybody else? OK, maybe not a hundred years, but a lot of years, and still there is only half electricity. Now, the nearest town, why, that's up to Ravensworth, about thirty miles away—'

'That's probably enough information, Lizzie.'

'So you two live in Blackbird Tree?'

'That's right,' Lizzie said. 'Naomi has been here for ever and a day, but I've only been here two years. Two years and one month. I live with the Cupwrights, who are going to adopt me. Are you an adopted boy?'

If you wanted to keep any secrets, you sure did not want Lizzie Scatterding to know all your business.

'Where's the school at in this Blackbird Creek place?'

'Tree,' I said. 'Blackbird *Tree*.'

'What's a blackbird tree, anyway?'

'You don't know what a blackbird tree is? Everybody knows that.' An ant had crawled up inside my shirt and was itching me. 'Tell him, Lizzie.'

'It's a tree shaped like a blackbird.'

'Lizzie, you crawdad. It is not.'

'Is too.'

'It's a tree full of blackbirds. Like the one at the bend. It's nearly always full of blackbirds. That's how the town got its name.'

'Are you sure about that?' Lizzie said.

'Of course I'm sure. Besides, it sounds a lot better than a town being named after a tree shaped like a blackbird, which there is not one of in this whole town or probably in the whole world.'

Finn handed Lizzie a stick. 'Draw me a map of this here Blackbird Tree town. Show me where we are and where you all live and if there's some kind of store, like for soda pop and pickles and nails and stuff.'

And so Lizzie did. Right there in the dirt, she drew a map of Blackbird Tree. She added some things I wouldn't have bothered with, like Crazy Cora's house and Witch Wiggins's place, in addition to my house and hers and Tebop's General Store. It about killed me to stay up in the tree because I would've drawn that map differently. She had things too close to each other and out of proportion, like Tebop's General Store was a giant square, about ten times as big as any house, when everybody who has a brain knows that Tebop's is barely a shack. I would've drawn it tiny and leaning over, about to fall into the road.

Finn studied the map for some time. Finally he said, 'I think I've got it in my head now.' He stood up and headed off. 'Best go,' he said. 'Ta.'

Lizzie raised a hand. 'Ta.'

Once Finn was long gone, I said, 'Ta'? What's this *ta* business? Since when did you start saying *ta*?'

'Since that Finn boy did,' she said. 'Are you going to stay up there all night, Naomi?'

'No, I am not.' I climbed down, landing right on top of the dirt sketch of Crazy Cora's house.

For my sixth birthday, Nula gave me a doll she had made. It had such a friendly face; the body was soft and squishy; her hair was curly and red, silky and fine. She wore a simple white cotton dress and black felt shoes. I named her Sophia and adored her instantly. I remember saying to Nula, 'Everything is different with Sophia here now. Everything!' And everything *was* different because I took her everywhere and told her everything and saw everything new through her eyes.

That's how everything felt now that Finn was here, as if everything was different.

CHAPTER 12

Another Stranger

Although the chickens behaved well enough with me, Joe and Nula, they didn't like too many others and could create a ruckus if approached. They had scratched and pecked a rutty mess in the yard as they roamed and clucked, *awk, awk*. Miss Johnny, the loner, ran here and there like a crazy person, calling out, *ooka, ooka*, in a high-pitched sound, unlike any other chicken I'd ever heard. I'd named the chickens, which annoyed Joe, partly because I'd given them all men's names, so I had to add 'Miss' to them: Miss Johnny, Miss Roy, Miss Danny, Miss Franklin – like that.

It was while I was thinking about the chickens and their voices that I realized what had been puzzling me about Finn. When we first met him, he had sounded different, a little strange. He'd talked in a way not completely odd to my ears but definitely not a Blackbird Tree way of talking, with our drawled-out middles of words. Finn spoke in a more lilting way, so that some words sat up and floated in the air.

Standing there in the chicken yard, I realized that Finn had sounded a little like Nula. The next time we saw Finn, though, he sounded more Blackbird Tree–like. He'd said, 'Where's the school at?' and *where's* sounded like *wahrrrz*, and *everything* sounded like *everthang*, which was the way you said things in Blackbird Tree.

When I mentioned this to Lizzie later in the day, she said, 'He *did* sound peculiar, but I thought it was because he was injured half to death.'

'But where's he from? That's what I'd like to know. He never did bother to answer that question.'

'What with school out and all, and with the dim Dimmenses never coming to school anyway, we may never see that Finn boy again, Naomi. Unless you want to try going up Black Dog Night Hill again. I don't think we ought to, though, do you? What with the dogs and all. I mean the other dogs, not the black dog with the yellow eyes, although that black dog would be reason enough not to go.'

'I'm not going back up the hill. I don't care if we never see that Finn boy again, anyway.' This was not the truth. I was desperate to see that Finn boy again. It was embarrassing to consider, but that's the way it was – as if I'd been hypnotized, and Finn boy had infiltrated my brain like a virus.

'I don't care, either,' Lizzie said. 'If you don't care, I don't care.'

As we walked to Tebop's General Store, we talked about our

summer. Lizzie's foster parents, the Cupwrights, and Nula and Joe were still in shock that we were out of school, and they had not yet pinned us down to chores. Usually we had about a week until they figured out we were on the loose, and that week was running out.

We would each have home chores, and the Cupwrights always made Lizzie do a volunteer project 'to help the community and people less fortunate.' Usually, I joined her because that got me out of more chores at Joe and Nula's and gave me more time hanging out with Lizzie.

At Tebop's store, several women were clustered around Mrs Tebop at the counter. *Buzz, buzz*, like busy flies.

'Glory! Who was he?'

'What'd you say his name was?'

'Dangle? Doodle?'

'I think it was—'

'Well, what'd he want?'

'Why would he drop in here, like an alien or something?'

'I have no—'

'He said he was interested—'

'In what? What was he interested in?'

'Sounds pretty nosy, if you ask me.'

'—the area. He was interested in "the lovely surrounds", that's the way he put it, kind of queerlike. And he talked funny.'

'Like how?'

Buzz, buzz.

What Lizzie and I put together was that a 'dapper man' had come into Tebop's, asking a lot of questions: How many people lived in the town? Were there any boarding houses? What were some nice places to visit? Was there a river? Did people fish there?

'Well, I'll be a nutberry!' Lizzie said as we left the store. 'First there's the Finn boy dropping out of nowhere, and now there's a Dangle Doodle man. Maybe next we will get a kangaroo hopping down the road. It's like *The Great Unexpected*.'

'What's that?'

'That's on the summer book list. *The Great Unexpected*. I hear it's way too long and too hard.'

The Great Unexpected. It sounded like my life, if you took the *great* out.

CHAPTER 13

Across the Ocean: A Visitor

Mrs Kavanagh

'Sybil, you've a visitor...' Pilpenny stopped to catch her breath.

'I've had enough of visitors.'

'And you won't like this one. I'm as sure of that as I am of my mother's grave.'

'Paddy McCoul, is it?'

'The very same.'

'Best hide me in the garden shed then.'

'He's already seen you. Look there, don't stare, see him by the roses?'

Mrs Kavanagh peered around Pilpenny. 'Ach. Paddy McCoul in the flesh. Best get me the gun.'

'Oh, Sybil.

'The axe?'

CHAPTER 14

Witch Wiggins

Lizzie and I were coming down Pork Street on our way home from Tebop's store, still talking about the stranger Dangle Doodle, when I saw Finn, up ahead, leaving Witch Wiggins's house. My heart was hopping around like a frog. I couldn't speak. I pulled on Lizzie's sleeve.

'Naomi, stop that. This is my only cardigan with all its buttons and you are stretching— Whoa. Whoa. Look at *that*. It's that Finn boy coming out of Witch Wiggins's house, oh heavens and stars.'

Finn waved. 'Hey, tree girls.'

Lizzie wagged her finger at Finn. 'Finn boy, I know you are new here and all, but you have to be careful where you go. Do you have any idea who lives in that house?'

'A lady by the name of Hazel.'

'*Hazel?*' Lizzie looked at Finn as if he were speaking

Turkish. 'That is the dwelling of Witch Wiggins, who has been known to eat boys bigger than you, so you are lucky to be alive.'

'She eats boys? Is that so?'

'Don't you know you have to stay clear of witches? What made you go in there in the first place? I am worried about you, Finn boy. Did you eat or drink anything while you were in there?'

'I had a couple biscuits – tasted kind of strange, I s'pose. And a glass or two of something red-coloured.'

Lizzie put her hand on Finn's forehead. 'How do you feel?'

'A little odd, I s'pose.'

'Naomi, he's feeling odd, and he ate strange biscuits and drank red liquids.'

'Lizzie, I am standing right here and I'm not deaf.'

'I'm feeling a little dizzy,' Finn said.

Lizzie leaped into action. 'Here, here, put your arm on my shoulder, that's right.'

I felt it necessary to get on the other side of Finn. 'Put your other arm here,' I said.

The three of us made our clumsy way down the street, and I have to say that it was a nice feeling having Finn's arm on my shoulder. We settled him on a bench at the corner of Pork and Main. Lizzie and I sat on either side of him to prop him up.

'So, what did you see inside Witch Wiggins's house, Finn boy?'

'Lots of things. About a thousand birds—'

'Dead or alive?' I asked.

'Alive.'

'How can there be a thousand alive birds in there?' Lizzie said. 'Where do they all fit? Why don't we hear a ton of birdsong? Is there bird slop every which way?'

Finn's left leg was about twenty centimetres from my right one. His left elbow was touching my right elbow. *Touching it.*

'I saw five or ten coffins,' Finn said.

'Open or closed?' I asked.

'Closed.'

'People-sized?' Lizzie asked. 'Where'd she get all those coffins? Are they empty or inhabited? Oh, Naomi, he saw coffins in there. *Coffins.* A thousand birds and *coffins.*'

'Yes, Lizzie, I believe my ears heard that.'

Finn abruptly stood up, shook his head around as if he were tossing off flies, and said, 'Thanks for the help. Have to go now.'

I didn't want him to go. I couldn't bear for him to leave. I wanted to grab hold of his shirt and beg him to stay. And then I was embarrassed for being such a drip over a boy. I was glad no one could see into my head.

Lizzie said, 'Wait, Finn boy. Are you sure you're well enough to be walking around on your own? Where are you going? Do you want help?'

'I'll be fine. Going up here a ways, to Miss Cora's house.'

I thought the top of Lizzie's head was going to fly open. 'Finn boy! You can't go there. That's Crazy Cora. You absolutely should not go there. That's *Crazy Cora*. Naomi, Finn boy is going to Crazy Cora's. Tell him he can't go there.'

I looked at Finn. He looked at me.

'Lizzie,' I said. 'I think this here Finn boy is going to go wherever he wants to go.'

'Well! I certainly do hope that this here Finn boy knows that we will not always be available to come to his rescue.'

I was thinking, I will. I *will always and ever be available to come to his rescue.*

Lizzie and the Cupwrights lived up closer to town, so Lizzie was a town girl and I was almost a country girl. I liked being away from things a bit. I wouldn't have liked it if every nosy body was strolling past our front porch looking at us and what was hanging on the clothesline.

In the kitchen, Nula was at the counter, pulling mixing bowls out of the cupboard. 'There you are, you lazy girl. Where are my eggs? Out with the chickens, I am supposing. Fetch me those eggs, you hear me? Here I am waiting for you to bring me the gossip, but first you fetch the eggs and then you can start the corn bread while you tell me the news.'

When I returned with the eggs, Nula sat at the table with an *oof*. 'You work, you talk and I will sit for the first five minutes all day, won't I?'

First I told her about the *buzz, buzz* at Tebop's General Store.

'Dapper?' Nula asked. 'They said he was a *dapper* man? That wouldn't be a Blackbird Tree man, now would it? Maybe a New York Big City man?'

'They said he talked funny.'

'Those New York Big City people talk funny.'

'They thought his name was Doodle or Dangle or something like that.'

'Probably a New York City reporter poking his nose into the ways of country folk. I don't see why Mrs Tebop gets in such a flap over the littlest things.'

Then I told Nula about seeing Finn coming out of Witch Wiggins's house.

'Finn? Ah, yes, Finn, the boy who fell out of the tree. You shouldn't call old Mrs Wiggins a witch, Naomi, even if she does have that warty nose and ear-splitting cackle and even if she does seem to affect the electricity in town.'

Whenever Witch Wiggins gets in a tussle with someone, the power goes out for hours.

Then I told Nula about Finn going on to Crazy Cora's house.

'That boy Finn gets around, doesn't he? How does he know so many people here?' Nula leaned towards the bowl in which I had gathered the cornbread ingredients. 'Naomi, did you put in that little bit of sugar the way I like?'

'I did.'

'That's fine, then. Now, where did you say this boy Finn went after the Wiggins place? Crazy Cora's? You really shouldn't call her crazy just because she has lost her mind entirely. She can't help it.'

Joe came in the back, letting the screen door slam shut. 'Who can't help it? Who are you talking about now?'

Nula said, 'Get on over here and rub my poor feet, old man.'

'Your poor feet? What about my achin' back?'

'*Tch*, sit on down. Here is the scoop, according to Naomi: a big-city dapper stranger was nosing around in Tebop's store, and that boy Finn—'

'What boy Finn?'

'The one that fell out of the tree. That boy Finn was over at Mrs Wiggins's place—'

'Witch Wiggins?'

'*Mrs Wiggins*. And then that boy Finn went on over to Cora Capolini's—'

'Crazy Cora's?' Joe slipped his hands inside the bib of his overalls and rested them on his chest. 'I certainly am glad that all these strangers have time to go nosing around and visiting while the rest of us are hard at work. Yes, sir, that gives me great comfort indeed.'

'Speaking of which,' Nula said, 'work, that is. Naomi, it seems to me you've had enough lollypogging around this week and we need to settle on your summer chores.'

'Rats,' I said. 'Poor, pitiful me.'

CHAPTER 15

The Barn

In the middle of Nula and Joe's property, between the house and the ploughed fields, squatted an old red barn. No longer used for animals or hay, it was home to: Joe's tractor; oil and gas cans; discarded furniture and appliances and saddles; a broken sundial; storage trunks; ladders; tools and gadgets of all shapes and sizes, including hoes, rakes, axes, hammers, shovels, screws, nails, tar pots, sandpaper, vices, saws and much, much more – toilet parts and rubber washers and wire snakes – basically anything you might need to fix something.

Joe did not lay claim to being the best fixer-upper, but he could probably take credit for trying the hardest. Every spring he climbed up on the house roof and replaced shingles that had blown off in the winter, and every winter they blew off again, and every spring he got back up there. The toilet was sometimes fixed with twine or dental floss or duct tape. Near every hook was a hole or two where he'd put a screw or nail in the wrong place first. Pretty much nothing hung level, but Joe said that was because one of his legs was shorter than the other and things that looked level to him might not look level to the rest of us.

Nula and Joe had decided that, in addition to my usual indoor chores and my chicken chores, my summer job would be to clean out the barn.

'The whole barn?'

Joe said, 'Yep.'

'The loft, too?'

'Yep.'

'That spidery place where the old reins and saddles are?'

'Yep.'

Joe said he'd find me some help when it came to the bigger appliances and that we'd take those to the junkyard. Other things we'd sell in a big yard sale and I could keep half the profits.

'Even if we get, say, a hundred dollars?'

'Yep.'

'I could keep half of that?'

'Yep.'

I had a sudden, sick feeling. 'Wait. The loft. What about – you know – the *trunks*?'

Nula put her hand to her mouth.

'What about 'em?' Joe said. 'Which trunks you talking about?'

Nula patted his arm. 'You know, the *trunks*. The *trunks*.' She blinked at him meaningfully.

'Ahhh,' he said. 'The *trunks*.' He tapped his fingers against his chest. 'Maybe now is a good time to deal with those trunks. We'll do it together. Not first, not right away. Maybe when everything else is done. How 'bout that? And if those trunks give us any trouble, we'll just kick 'em. How 'bout that?'

I was reminded of Joe's tale of the poor man who won a donkey, and out of the donkey's ears the man pulled astonishing things. One of my worries about the trunks in the barn was that they would be like my worst fears about the donkey's ears: instead of something good coming out of them, we might pull out something bad.

CHAPTER 16

Across the Ocean: The Request

Mrs Kavanagh

Mrs Kavanagh watched as Paddy McCoul appro- ached slowly, tentatively, his hat in hand, looking down at his feet as if he had something to be ashamed of – which he did, he did. He was of middling height and stocky, with ruddy cheeks and thick, unruly, greying hair. His clothes were ill-fitting: his shirt and jacket too tight, his trousers baggy. He looked like a man who needed some tending.

Serves him right, thought Mrs Kavanagh. She waited for him to speak first. She was not going to make this easy for him.

'Sybil—er—Ma'am—er—Missus—'

Mrs Kavanagh looked up at him, eyeing him as if he were a curious donkey who had wandered into the orchard.

'Not sure what to call you. You was always Sybil to me, and then once't you come up to the Master's house – God rest his soul in heaven above—I didn'—I don'—'

'Stop your yabbering, Paddy McCoul. You don't need to call me anything at all. You don't need to be here at all. State your business and be off with you.'

Paddy twisted the hat in his hand. 'Now, Sybil, er, Missus – is that any way to talk to an old friend?'

'Pilpenny!' Mrs Kavanagh shouted towards the house. 'Bring the gun!'

'Now, now, no need to let tempers flare—'

'You'd best state your business quick, Paddy McCoul. Pilpenny! The big gun!'

'*Och.* Yes'm, yes'm. I come for the trunk.'

'What trunk?'

'The one, ma'am, of me only son—' Paddy McCoul pulled a soiled rag – not even a handkerchief, Mrs Kavanagh noticed – from his pocket and dabbed at his eyes.

'Stop the foolery, Paddy McCoul. You won't get my sympathy. You're a useless wreck of a man and you don't deserve even the dust that lies on that trunk. You'd best be off before – Pilpenny! Ah, here comes Pilpenny with my gun.'

Paddy McCoul backed away. 'This is no way to treat me, Sybil. You'd best think it over. I'll be seeing a solicitor, I will.'

'Fine indeed. Lovely, that. You see a solicitor, Paddy McCoul, and if he does not laugh you out of his office, I will be a dinneky doon.'

'A what?'

Mrs Kavanagh took the gun from Pilpenny and placed it across her lap. With one end of her shawl, she dusted off the muzzle. She raised the gun.

CHAPTER 17

The Unfortunate Souls

Lizzie's home chores were few because Mrs Cupwright suffered headaches when 'persons' were underfoot, and so Lizzie offered to help me clean out the barn if I would help with her community service. The target of her service to the community was going to be 'the unfortunate elderly', under the supervision of Mrs Mudkin, from her church.

Joe, Nula and I did not go to an official church on Sunday, much to the botherment of others. Instead, we had 'Sunday pause' time. After Sunday breakfast, we'd go outside and sit ourselves down wherever we chose – on the fence, the ground, or the metal chairs – and Joe would say something along the lines of, 'Look at this green place we have landed in. It's a beauty,' and Nula would say, 'It's almost as green as the green hills of Ireland,' and I would usually not say anything at all, merely listen to the chickens or the birds or the church bells in the distance.

We'd sit there awhile, depending on the weather, until Joe would say, 'There, now. That feels good and I didn't even have to put on fancy clothes.'

I used to enjoy these Sunday pauses, but for the past year they'd been making me itchy. *What else?* I wondered. *What else is out there?* And I would fly off, up into the air, through the clouds, over the fields, beyond the town, over the cities, over the rivers, over the ocean until I got to the green hills of Ireland, and when I heard Joe say, 'There, now. That feels good . . . ' I'd come home.

On Sunday afternoon, I met Lizzie at her church so we could go over our duties with Mrs Mudkin for helping the poor, unfortunate elderly. If you saw Mrs Mudkin, you might wonder why she herself was not on the list of the poor, unfortunate elderly. Tiny and narrow as a stick, she had papery skin so thin you could see right through to her veins. On her face, as wrinkled as an old plum, were narrow glasses dotted with rhinestones. Her hair was violet and tightly curled; her brown-flowered dress fell to her tightly laced, sturdy shoes.

She was not sure if I would be a good helper for Lizzie, seeing as I did not belong to their church, but Lizzie told her that I might be converted if I hung around her doing good deeds for the poor, unfortunate elderly.

'Now, girls,' Mrs Mudkin said, 'here is a list of things you might do to help the poor souls.' She handed Lizzie a piece of paper on which she had written, in her shaky script, suggestions. She then proceeded to read the list to us:

'You might assist with personal grooming (combing hair, tying shoes, washing)—'

Lizzie interrupted. 'Washing? You don't mean bathing them, do you? Because I don't think that's appropriate, do you?'

'Well, now, no, dear,' Mrs Mudkin said. 'I mean maybe they want help washing their faces.'

'Excuse me, ma'am, but are you saying some of these souls are so unfortunate that they cannot wash their own faces?'

'Well, now. If they are bedridden, for example, they might need help with that, yes.' Mrs Mudkin glanced down at her list and read the second item. 'You might assist with household chores, such as dusting, sweeping, dishwashing, laundry, ironing.'

Lizzie said, 'Excuse me, ma'am, but that sounds like what a maid would do. Are we going to be maids for the poor, unfortunate souls?'

Mrs Mudkin eyed Lizzie over the top of her jewelled spectacles. 'No, you are not going to be maids. You might only do one or two of these things for each person. Here, dear, why don't you read through the list on your own, and I will meet you here Tuesday at noon and escort you to the first home. You'll find a list of poor, unfortunate souls on the back.'

Mrs Mudkin seemed in a hurry to be rid of us, nearly pushing us out of the door. At the bench outside of Tebop's store, we sat down to read through the rest of the list. Most of the suggestions were along the lines of: reading aloud from the newspaper or Bible, feeding cats and changing litter boxes, that sort of thing. At the bottom, though, was a note about Things to Avoid, and these included:

Discourage use of alcohol and tobacco.

Discourage bad language.

Discourage slovenly habits.

Lizzie turned the page over. On the back was a list of four names and their addresses. The first two were elderly gentlemen, Mr T. Canner of 12 Elm Street, and Mr A. Farley of 23 Pork Street.

'You know them, right, Naomi? The one with the pointy head – old man Canner? And the one who got hit by the train – one-armed Farley?'

And then we saw the next two names.

'No!' Lizzie breathed. 'No!'

But there they were, right there: both Crazy Cora and Witch Wiggins were on the list.

'We can't go there,' Lizzie said. 'We are just going to have to tell Mrs Mudkin, aren't we, Naomi? We can't be going into places that have a thousand live birds and a bunch of coffins and crazy people running about. We certainly can't be expected to go to *those* places, can we?'

❧

Once, when I was seven or eight, I climbed a tall oak tree at the far edge of our field. What a view! A breeze came in fits and starts, the leaves tickled my arms and legs and I was at the top of the world. As I went to climb down, my foot slipped and my weaker arm wasn't able to grab the nearest branch, and down, down I went. I remember thinking, *I'm falling, falling.* I came to at the base of the tree: scratched, bruised and with a powerful headache. I made my way to the house, where Joe greeted me.

'What got you? Have you been tangling with a bear? Fall out of a tree?'

'That was the other Naomi.'

'What?'

'Not me, the other Naomi. *She* fell out of a tree.'

Joe and Nula kidded me about that for some time. If I left the milk out on the counter, they'd say, 'Who left that milk out? Must've been the other Naomi,' or 'Did the other Naomi forget to feed the chickens?'

After we left Mrs Mudkin, I was wondering if maybe the other Naomi could visit the unfortunate souls.

CHAPTER 18

The Dangle Doodle Man

I was on my way home that day when I heard, 'Hey, tree girl!'

I turned round. Finn was floating towards me. Truly, I think he floated on the air. My feet stuck to the ground and my mouth froze in an O.

'Hey, tree girl, wait up.'

Wait up? I couldn't have moved even if I'd wanted to.

Look at that nice hair, I thought stupidly. *Look at those long legs. Look at that mouth . . .*

When he reached me, he said. 'I've got a question for you.'

I managed to form a few words. 'For me?'

'You seem to know everyone around here, so maybe you know this person.'

He smelled very, very good. Clean, like soap. 'Which person?'

'Elizabeth Scatterding.'

'Who?' I croaked.

'Elizabeth Scatterding. Do you know where I could find her?'

I wondered if a person could die standing up. 'That's Lizzie,' I finally managed. 'The other tree girl.'

Finn smiled and tapped my arm. 'Ho! You don't say! That's great. Where does she live?'

And so I, in my supreme mortification, had to tell Finn where my friend Lizzie Scatterdinghead lived, and then I had to watch him wave at me as he turned and headed in the direction of Lizzie's house, and then I had to force my body to aim for home, picking up my leaden feet one at a slow, glompy time.

My brain was shut down. It felt as if a fungus had infiltrated every little convoluted corner.

In the distance, a man was coming towards me. Definitely not a Blackbirdy Tree critter. He was a rectangle man – tall and narrow – and dressed up as if for church, with a suit and tie and shiny shoes.

'Hello there, miss,' he said in a most polite way. 'Miss' sat aloft in the air a few seconds. 'Charming day, don't you think?'

'Mmm.'

'I'm having a little stroll, obtaining my bearings.'

'Mmm.' *This must be the Dingle Dangle man*, I thought. *Odd that he and Finn have come to town at the same time.*

I said, 'You don't happen to know a boy named Finn, do you?'

His head jerked slightly to the left and then to the right, like a bird on a worm prowl.

'What's that? I beg your pardon?'

'A boy named Finn – do you happen to know him?' His

eyes switched from left to right. 'Finn? Did you say *Finn*?'

'I did.'

'Goodness. *Finn*, you say?' With one finger he stroked the top of his head. 'I've known a few Finns, more than a few to be precise.'

'But did you bring a boy named Finn here with you to Blackbird Tree?'

'Not that I recall.'

'Mmm. Well, if you're looking for a Finn, he's over at the Cupwrights visiting Miss Lizzie Scatterdinghead.'

'How perfectly odd,' the man said. 'And might I ask your name?'

'No.'

'I see. No matter. Ta.'

Nula was standing on the porch, hands on hips. 'Power's out. Who is ole Wiggins mad at now?'

'Don't know. Don't know anything today. Going up to the barn for a bit.'

From the barn, from the loft, I went to the moon. It took me a while to get there, but when I arrived, I opened my eyes and looked back at the earth. I did not see a beautiful blue-and-green marble. What I saw was a giant blow-up of Finn and Lizzie laughing together. Their faces were so big they blotted out the earth. I looked down at my feet. Red lava was swirling around them. Maybe I was on the wrong planet.

CHAPTER 19

A Family

On the wall in the barn loft was a faded drawing I'd made when I was five years old. Two tall stick figures with large heads were Joe and Nula; between them was me – a tiny child figure with a small head and an O for a mouth. To each side of the figures was a brown horizontal line to show the ground, and below that line on one side were two long, grey boxes, coloured with strong strokes going every which way. A single flower grew out of each box. Beneath the drawing, in my childish handwriting, was: *My Family*.

I had no recollection of my mother, of course, and only a faint one of my father. I do not remember the events of 'the day of the dog,' but I do remember the fear. I know only what has been told to me.

My father and I lived in a small cabin at the back of Joe and Nula's property. I was three years old, playing in the yard, chasing a chicken. My father was sitting on the porch steps, stringing beans. From out of nowhere a stray dog bounded into the yard, sending the chickens flapping. Apparently I squealed, thinking this was a game, and ran towards the dog. The dog must have been spooked, or maybe it thought I was a big chicken. It lunged at me, catching my arm in its jaws and flinging me left and right.

My father saved me from the dog but was badly bitten in the process. We both were hospitalized. I was released to Joe and Nula a week later, but my father never left the hospital. He died there.

I once heard Nula explain this to one of my teachers. 'She didn't have anybody else, did she? We were going to look after her until somebody who might be related to her showed up, but nobody ever did.'

I couldn't tell how Nula felt about this arrangement. Nula didn't sound happy and she didn't sound angry, but from then on I wondered what would happen if someone showed up one day and claimed me. Would Nula and Joe have to – or want to – hand me over?

For several years, there were photos of my parents in my bedroom. Nula used to say to me, 'This is your mother, and this is your father,' and I could readily point to these photos and repeat 'mother' and 'father', but that's all the association I had. To me, 'mother' and 'father' were photographs. I could have clipped faces of two strangers from magazines and framed them. Mother. Father.

A photograph in Nula's room showed a young Nula, maybe seven years old, with an older sister. The two of them looked so much alike. They wore coarse dresses and were barefoot and had their arms wrapped around each other and smiled freely into the camera.

'That was before I was sent away,' Nula once said.

'Sent away? Why?'

Nula's face took on a hard look. 'Because we had nothing,' she said, 'and those who had nothing – no food, no milk, no clothing beyond what we had on, no money at all – those who had nothing could be sent, or given, away.'

I worried over this information. 'We have food, don't we, Nula? We have some money, don't we?'

'Today we do, yes. Today we have food and a roof over our heads.'

'And tomorrow?'

'Tomorrow,' Nula said, 'is tomorrow.'

Nula used to read to me. I remember especially a series of tales in which a boy and girl could become various beings – bear, fox, eagle – merely by wishing it so. One morning, Nula showed me a book of dinosaurs and other prehistoric creatures, the most appealing of which was a pteranodon, a flying reptile, and later that day I announced that I was going to become a pteranodon.

'A pteranodon?' Nula said. 'My, my. And how will that happen?'

'I'll wish it.'

'You will, will you?'

I closed my eyes and said, 'I wish, I wish, with all my might, to be a pteranodon.'

When I opened my eyes, Nula said, 'Guess it didn't work.'

'Not yet. In the *morning* I will be a pteranodon. I will be able to fly. I will fly, fly – I wonder where I will live?'

I must have gone on like that for some time because eventually Nula said, 'Naomi, you know you won't *really* wake up as a pteranodon, don't you?'

'But I will. I wish it with all my might.'

'You can't actually turn into a pteranodon—'

'I can! I will! I wish, I wish, with all my might—'

'You won't. I'm sorry, but you won't. You can wish it, but you will not be able to turn into a pteranodon.'

I was inconsolable, as if it were Nula herself who was preventing me from obtaining my wish.

When I woke the next morning and saw that I was not, in fact, a pteranodon, I felt as if I was also no longer the Naomi who had gone to bed the night before. I was different, Nula and Joe were different, the world was different. I think this is when I knew absolutely that I had no mother and no father and I would never have them again.

A year or two later a teacher read a story about a young knight on a quest. I remember none of the story except that the description of the knight's shining armour and his sturdy horse and the golden woods drew me in, and while the teacher read,

I *was* the knight on the horse riding through the golden wood. I was that knight as surely as I was ever anyone else. I saw what he saw, felt what he felt, and when the teacher stopped reading, I could not move because I was still in the book. Unable to rouse me from that dreamy state, the teacher sent for Nula.

I told Nula the story of the knight and his glimmering armour and the golden woods. She said, 'Naomi, you know that is a story, don't you?'

'But what is "a story"? It's in here now' – I tapped my head – 'with all the other stuff, so maybe everything is a story.'

That night, I went to sleep supremely happy. If I could be a knight, then I could be a pteranodon, or I could be an eagle or a bear or a fox, or anything at all, and I could dwell where I pleased and do what I pleased, and if I wanted to have a mother, I could have a mother, and if I wanted to have a father, I could have a father. I could do and be and have all these things; I could be anywhere and everywhere.

CHAPTER 20

Finns

At dinner, we had sandwiches because the power was still out. 'That Witch Wiggins,' Joe said. 'Somebody must've riled her up good. Maybe it was that Finn boy of yours, that one who fell out of a tree. You seen any more of that boy?'

'Yes, and you know what he wanted to know? He wanted to know where Elizabeth Scatterding lived. *Elizabeth!*'

'That's Lizzie's full name?'

'Yes. Elizabeth Scatterdinghead.'

'My, my,' Nula said. 'Am I hearing a wee bit of bother?'

'What's he doing calling her *Elizabeth* and how does he know that's her real name and why does he want to know where she lives? Not that I care.'

'No, no, why would you care?' Nula said. 'Shall I tell you about the Finn I knew? He sounds like your Finn, he does. Do you know your Finn's last name?'

'He's not my Finn, and no, I don't know his last name.'

The lights flickered; the power was back on. Nula did not seem to notice.

'Let me tell you about *my* Finn, Finn McCoul, though Finn wasn't even his real name, but that's another story. So into Duffayn one bright summer's day strolls a handsome young lad, calls himself Finn McCoul, and doesn't he flatter me, and doesn't he not notice me dirty smock or me bare feet? And doesn't he bring the meadow flowers and doesn't he say he will come into money when he is sixteen, so much money, and land, too? Doesn't he say so?'

Joe was nodding as if he had heard this before.

Nula's chin rested on the fingertips of one hand, daintily.

'And doesn't he notice me older sister, too, and doesn't he flatter her, and doesn't he bring her meadow flowers and tell her he will come into money and land in two years' time, doesn't he say so?'

Joe says, 'The charmer.'

'The charmer indeed, indeed. I thought him such a fine young lad and I was blinkered.'

'Blinkered?'

'I could not see properly. He turned out not to be a fine young lad, didn't he, that Finn McCoul, and his name was not even properly Finn.'

'What was it?'

'Paddy. Paddy McCoul.'

The lights blinked; the power went out again.

That night, after I'd gone to bed, Nula leaned into the room. "Night, Naomi lass, and don't think about that Finn boy. Put him out of your mind.'

'Who? I don't know who you are talking about.'

'Good.'

I closed my eyes and despite my best efforts, one word and one face swirled around my head: *Finn, Finn, Finn, Finn, Finn, Finn, Finn.*

CHAPTER 21

Across the Ocean: The Bridge

Mrs Kavanagh

Pilpenny wheeled Mrs Kavanagh's chair to the edge of the Crooked Bridge, which crossed, in its zigzag fashion, a narrow river. Mrs Kavanagh's dogs, Sadie and Maddie, had run on ahead.

'How clear the water is today, Pilpenny. So refreshing, don't you think?'

'Yes, 'tis. You can see every pebble, every minnow.'

'Are you ready, Pilpenny? Faster than last time, if you can.'

Pilpenny bent her knees and set off trotting behind the wheelchair, swerving at each sharp turn of the bridge. Left, right, right, left, right, left.

'Whoopsie, don't send me through the rails, Pilpenny.'

''Twould serve you right, you goose.'

'Whoo!'

Once on the other side, it took the women a few minutes to slow their breathing.

'That silly old Master,' Mrs Kavanagh said at last. 'I don't think this foolish bridge saved him from the evil spirits in the end, do you, Pilpenny? The evil spirits would have to be terribly dim to fall off the turns as he had hoped.'

'The stars shone on his son, though, didn't they, Sybil? Albert was nothing like the Master, thanks be.'

'Ah. Albert. Sweet Albert.' Sybil raised her left hand, adorned only by a simple gold band. 'Nothing like his father the Master. Sweet Albert.'

At the entry to the orchard stood an elegant wrought-iron gate flanked by two tall iron pillars. Perched atop each pillar was a black iron rook. Pilpenny pushed the wheelchair along the centre path, past the aged apple, plum and pear trees, past the sundial and the fairy ring. The trees were in full leaf, the young fruit small. The dogs circled in and out, chasing squirrels and baying at trees.

When the two women paused at the end of the path, Mrs Kavanagh gestured towards the meadow beyond. 'There, I think. That would be a good spot, don't you agree, Pilpenny? If all goes well. I am eager to hear from Dingle. Perhaps tomorrow he will phone.'

CHAPTER 22

I Don't Care

One of the first things I decided when I woke up on Monday morning was that I was not going over to Lizzie's. She could come to me. I was not going to ask about Finn. She could tell me in her good old time. I was not going to appear interested. I didn't care.

I fed the chickens.

I didn't care.

I told Nula that I was going to begin cleaning the barn.

I didn't care.

I walked into the barn, turned round, went back to the house, told Nula I had a quick errand to do and took off for Lizzie's, running, until I was a block away, and then I slowed to a walk.

Be calm, I told myself.

Mr Cupwright came to the door. He said Lizzie wasn't home.

'Where is she?'

'Don't know. None of my business.'

'But she's your...' I took a step backwards. 'I don't suppose you happen to know if a boy named Finn came by here yesterday?'

'Who?'

'Finn.'

'Thin?'

'Finn. *Ffff-inn.*'

'Don't know. None of my business.'

I stomped all the way home.

I don't care. I don't care. I don't care. I don't care.

As I passed Tebop's store, I wondered why people had made such a fuss about the stranger Dangle Doodle but no one had mentioned the stranger boy Finn yet, at least not that I had heard.

'Kids,' Mrs Tebop liked to say, 'are supposed to be invisible.'

I don't care. I don't care. I don't care.

CHAPTER 23

The First Unfortunate Soul

For the assault on our first unfortunate soul, Lizzie and I met Mrs Mudkin at her church and walked from there to old man Canner's house on Elm Street. Lizzie had not said one word about Finn's visiting her on Sunday, and I was getting mighty rattled. She acted as if nothing whatsoever were wrong.

'Lar-de-dar,' she sang. 'Mr T. Canner, lar-de-dar, we are coming for you, lar-de-dar.'

Lizzie was walking alongside frail Mrs Mudkin to hold her upright.

'Now, girls,' Mrs Mudkin said, 'I will be right there with you until you get settled. Then I will be next door visiting—'

'Wait. You're leaving us *alone* here?' I asked.

'If you need me, ring that bell I gave you.'

I was carrying a clunky school bell, about as big as a sheep's head and sporting a wooden handle with a chunk out of it from when Mrs Mudkin must have clonked one of her students when she was a teacher back in the very old days.

Mr Canner sat in a musty chair with tufts of stuffing sticking out like a sloppy bird's nest. He had a pinched face, like a dried-up olive, a pointy head and tiny glittering eyes. I can't hardly describe what he was wearing. It looked like a costume from an old-time movie: a blue shirt with a stiff white collar, a grey waistcoat and plaid trousers with sharp pleats tucked into shiny brown lace-up boots. He was not big on pleasantries.

'Lace up my boots,' he said, before we had been introduced.

Mrs Mudkin nodded at me, so I got down and started lacing up the boots.

'Not too tight,' he warned. 'Not too loose, neither.'

When Mrs Mudkin explained why we were there, Mr Canner looked up at her as if she were a stray animal that had wandered in.

'What would they want to do *here*?' he asked.

'Why, I have explained that, Mr Canner. Lizzie and Naomi are here to help you.'

'I don't need no help.'

'They could read to you,' Mrs Mudkin suggested.

'I can't hear nothin'.'

'Now, now, Mr Canner, you seem to hear me fine,' Mrs Mudkin cooed.

'What? What's that you said?'

'Mercy! These girls are here for an hour and they are going to help you whether you like it or not.' She turned to us. 'There you go, girls. I'll be right next door.'

Mrs Mudkin had no sooner closed the door behind her than Mr Canner let out a loud belch. 'That woman gives me indigestion.' He blinked at us for a few minutes and then said, 'I suppose one of you could do up the breakfast dishes and the other could read a little, unless you're those snotty kind of lazy kids.'

Lizzie headed for the kitchen. I studied the bookshelves.

'Anything in particular you want me to read?' I asked.

He motioned towards the table nearest him. 'One of these. You can choose.'

I examined a leather volume with green etching on the cover: *Short Tales from Around the World*. The print was not too small and there was fair space between the lines and that suited me. For an hour I read while Mr Canner leaned his head against the back of the chair and listened. In the kitchen, we could hear Lizzie clanking dishes and singing, 'Lar-de-dar, lar-de-dar.'

We didn't have to use Mrs Mudkin's bell to ring for help, and the time was up before I realized it, so caught up was I in the tale of an Irish ogre and then in the tale of a fox and some chickens, and such. We told Mr Canner we'd be back the following Tuesday at the same time, and he nodded. I thought he'd be more excited about that, but if he was, he hid it well.

As soon as we were outside, though, my first thought was Finn. *Finn and Lizzie.*

'Lar-de-dar, that was easier than I thought it would be, don't you think so, too, Naomi? And the poor, unfortunate soul, why, there were two days' worth of dishes in that sink, all dried-up and crusty. He never would have been able to get them as clean as I did. Won't he be surprised when he sees how I cleaned off the table and got rid of all those old papers and swept the floor, and I mopped it, too, Naomi, because truly, the poor, unfortunate soul would never be able to do that for himself, now, would he? And doesn't it make your heart ache so for the poor, elderly people who are falling apart every which way, and—'

'Lizzie! Stop! Take a breath. Don't you have something to tell me?'

Lizzie crossed her hands over her chest. 'Why, Naomi Deane, whatever do you mean? What is it? What do I have to tell you?' She beamed at me, as if I was going to tell her a secret.

Sometimes, truly, I wanted to put a sack over Lizzie's head.

CHAPTER 24

The Second Unfortunate Soul

Mrs Mudkin called to us from the house next door to Mr Canner's. 'Girls, come and give me a hand, we're late, don't you know, late! We have another unfortunate soul to attend to.'

'Today?' I didn't think we'd have to do two in one day. I felt as if my head would jump right off my neck if I couldn't find out what happened with Finn and Lizzie.

'Of course today. Lizzie, didn't you make that clear to Neema?'

'Naomi. *Nay-oh-me.*'

Off we marched to Pork Street, where one-armed Farley lived in a room at the back of Mrs Broadley's boarding house. As we climbed the porch steps, the door swung open and the dapper Dangle Doodle man stepped out.

'Ladies!' he said, bowing as he held the door open.

Mrs Mudkin pulled Lizzie inside and reached back to grab my arm. '*Foreigner*,' she whispered.

The hallway smelled of mothballs.

Crammed into one-armed Farley's room was a tall four-poster bed draped with a green-and-white quilt; a blue velvet sofa and matching large armchair; an enormous glass-fronted cabinet filled with china and glassware; a tall dark dresser; two dining chairs and a round wooden table covered with a lace tablecloth; and fragile knickknacks: china figurines, glass paperweights, delicate bowls. We might as well have wandered into an antique shop.

'Golly,' Lizzie said, 'you surely have some beautiful things in here, don't you, Mr Farley? I never expected to see so many colourful, large things in this small space.'

'It ain't mine.'

Now, I could have guessed that. Everyone in town knew that one-armed Farley had been a whisky-drinking, cigar-smoking man of questionable character. People said he'd been fired from every job he ever had, and he'd been tossed out of every diner and bar in a thirty-mile radius. One night he fell down drunk on a railroad track and didn't even wake up when the 4:00 a.m. freight train ran over his arm.

In the hospital up in Ravensworth, he met a woman named Mary-Mary, and he found love and religion and was pretty nearly reformed (according to Mrs Mudkin) until he learned that Mary-Mary, far younger than he, was already happily married. He left Blackbird Tree for some time but returned three or four years ago, and ever since then, he had stayed in this room at Mrs Broadley's boarding house, leaving it only once a week when Mrs Broadley forced him out so she could clean the premises.

'None of this stuff is mine,' Mr Farley said. 'None of these fancy gewgaws, none of this furniture, none of these – these' – he flapped his hand at the lace table-cloth – 'these frippy things. It's all Mrs Broadley's. I think I'm living in her storage room.'

Mrs Mudkin explained to him why we were there.

'I cain't think of a single thang for them to do,' Mr Farley said, jerking his head towards me and Lizzie. He was a flabby, pale man with heavy, sagging cheeks and a bald head. He wore faded blue jeans, a red flannel shirt and brown slippers.

Mrs Mudkin surveyed the room. It was clean and dusted, the bed was made and everything was as tidy as if it had been prepared for company.

'They could read to you,' Mrs Mudkin offered.

'No, they cain't.'

'I'm saying they *could*, if you wanted them to.'

'No, they cain't. I'll stuff socks in my ears if they try it. I hate being read to. Makes me feel like a baby. I ain't no baby.'

'Mr Farley, sir,' Lizzie said, 'we would be most happy to take you out for a walk. It is such a beautiful day with the sun shining all around and the green leaves so plentiful on the trees—'

'Nope. Don't like walks.'

I wanted to bomp him on the head for being so stubborn. 'What *do* you like, Mr Farley?'

Mr Farley looked surprised. He opened his mouth and shut

it again without any words coming out. He looked as if no one had ever asked him that question before.

'I—I—' Mr Farley bent his head, leaned forward and covered his face with his hands. He appeared to be crying.

Mrs Mudkin, Lizzie and I stood there like frozen turkeys. I gazed into the china cabinet, wishing I were anywhere else but in that room. *Who eats off those dishes?* I wondered. *Is that a little Eiffel Tower statue?* On one shelf, between the dishes, were two iron birds, about ten centimetres high. *Crows, maybe.*

Mr Farley was saying something, but we couldn't make out what it was.

Lizzie put one finger on his shoulder. 'Mr Farley? What did you say?'

'Meetumking.'

'What's that, Mr Farley?'

'Meetumking.'

'I'm sorry, Mr Farley, but we can't quite understand—'

Mr Farley looked up abruptly. 'MEET THE KING! Are you deaf? I said I want to meet the King!'

'The King? What King?'

With considerable trial and error, we discovered that Mr Farley was desperate to meet the King of Ireland.

'Does Ireland have a king?' I asked. 'Are you sure?'

Mrs Mudkin turned to Lizzie. 'Does he want to go to Ireland? How is he going to do that?'

'HERE!' Mr Farley said. 'He is HERE.'

Mrs Mudkin moved towards the door and motioned for me and Lizzie to join her.

'I do believe,' Mrs Mudkin said, 'that the poor, unfortunate soul is having delusions, and I do not think that you girls should be left alone with him today. We will try again next week.'

Mrs Mudkin approached Mr Farley. 'We have to leave now—'

'Ireland? Are we going to Ireland?'

'No, Mr Farley—'

'Are you bringing the King?'

'Erm, the King? We are going to enquire about the King. Yes, we are going to see if we can locate him.'

In the hallway outside Mr Farley's room, Mrs Mudkin said, 'The poor soul has lost his marbles.' Her papery, thin fingers fluttered at her lips. 'Tragic, really. You two girls run along. I'll stop in to see if Mrs Broadley has any insights as to Mr Farley's unfortunate condition. Go on, and don't forget to meet me again on Thursday for our next two souls.'

Outside, Lizzie said, 'Gosh, Naomi, heavens above, that poor soul is hallucinating! I thought he might conjure up the devil himself. I thought—'

'Lizzie. Lizzie. STOP talking for two minutes. Catch a breath. Close your yap. Are you going to tell me what happened with Finn or what?'

'Finn? Why, Naomi, whatever has come over you?'

'Don't act so innocent, Lizzie. I happen to know that Finn went to your house on Sunday, so fess up.'

'He did? Finn came to *my* house? Whatever for? Do tell, Naomi, tell me all about it, oh, please, do.'

Surely my head flipped right up off my neck, wobbled and set itself back down. Maybe *I* was the one who was hallucinating.

CHAPTER 25

Of Lies and Such

One thing about Lizzie that was both reassuring and maddening was that she did not tell lies. She did not seem to know *how* to lie.

If Bo Dimmens asked you what you thought of the ridiculous, lime-coloured beret he had taken to wearing, you might want to tell a little fiction. You might want to say, 'Looks cool, Bo.' If you told the truth, Bo Dimmens might dump a bucket of lard on your head.

Lizzie, however, could not even tell that little lie and yet no one bopped her on the head. Why? Because she numbed people with an avalanche of words. She might say to Bo Dimmens, about his foolish hat, 'Why, Bo, what kind of hat is that on your head? What is that called, and does it keep your head warm and do you *want* it to keep your head warm in the *summer*, or mightn't it be better to have a cooler hat in the summer, or maybe I don't understand the purpose of that kind of hat, seeing as I've never seen one before.' Bo would be standing there showing the insides of his mouth, not knowing whether he had been insulted or complimented.

If Mrs Mudkin asked you if you thought her doddery, rickety, stick-thin, wrinkled self looked old, you might feel obliged to take your own flight of fancy and say, 'Surely not, Mrs Mudkin. You're a long way from looking *old*.' Otherwise, Mrs Mudkin might launch into a sermon about not insulting your elders.

But Lizzie might say to Mrs Mudkin, 'Of course you look old, Mrs Mudkin, but in the most beautiful of ways, what with all your charming wrinkles. I do hope I have wrinkles like that when I get old. It shows so much character, don't you think?'

Even if you thought stingy Alice Krupkins with her dripping nose and whining voice was the last person on earth you'd want to be stuck in a closet with, you couldn't actually tell her that, could you? You could *think* it, but you might not want to say it out loud or else she would hyperventilate and squeal and run to the nearest adults and inform them of your meanness.

But Lizzie would say to Alice Krupkins (and I know this for a fact), 'Alice, I am so entirely worried about you because your nose is running like a leaky cow udder, and perhaps you need to rest up and take some cod liver oil, which is what I take every day even though I do not like the smell of it one bit, but sometimes you have to make sacrifices for your health, don't you?'

The reason Lizzie's inability to lie was reassuring was that if you asked her a question, you knew she would always tell you the truth, even though she might take way too many words to tell that truth. The reason her inability to lie was also maddening was because you could not get away with your own little lies if Lizzie was around.

So, knowing that Lizzie was not able to lie, I was stumped as to why she was being so ignorant about Finn having gone to her house on Sunday.

'Truly, Naomi? Finn came to *my* house? I do wish you would tell me all about it.'

'I *know* that he came to your house. He *told* me that's where he was going. He asked me where you lived.'

'He *did*? Now, whyever did he do that, Naomi? Didn't I well and truly show him on the little dirt map I drew for him?'

'It's kind of hard to tell from scratches in the dirt exactly which house is which, Lizzie. Are you trying to say Finn did *not* come to your house on Sunday evening?'

'I surely do not know, Naomi, do I? If I knew that he came, I would know what you are talking about. And how would I know anyway since I was not home on Sunday evening? As you well and truly know, I was back at church.'

Sunday-night services. I'd forgotten. Naturally, I felt bad for thinking Lizzie was hiding something from me, but I still held a little something against her. I blamed her for Finn's wanting to go to her house in the first place.

I told Lizzie about running into Finn and his asking me where she lived. I tried to sound casual, as if it was not of any importance whatsoever.

'Naomi! Isn't that most interesting? I wonder why he would want to know where I lived. Did he want to know where anyone else lived? Isn't that peculiar? What a fascinating boy that Finn boy is, don't you think, Naomi?'

My tongue had become saturated with jealousy. I could not speak.

CHAPTER 26

Across The Ocean: The Call

MRS KAVANAGH

Mrs Kavanagh was in the orchard, her wheelchair parked comfortably in the shade, her feet resting on the back of one of her foxhounds. The other dog lay nose to nose with its sister. Both dogs slept comfortably, their ears and noses twitching occasionally at scents and sounds both dreamed and real.

Mrs Kavanagh was thinking about lies, small ones and large ones. Even the small ones had consequences, but then so did small truths. If you were twelve, say, and told your sister you'd never kissed a boy, it seemed a small lie, didn't it? But if that small lie was discovered, a sister's trust could be lost, and a sister's trust was worth more than the gold in a rich man's vault.

And so it had been with Mrs Kavanagh and her sister when

they were young and both of them charmed by the same boy, that wicked Paddy McCoul.

Mrs Kavanagh's reverie was interrupted by the appearance of Pilpenny.

'I have news, Sybil, you'll be pleased to hear.'

'And what is that, Pilpenny?'

'Your Mr Dingle has rung, quite cheery, and says there are some "interesting complications" – those are the words he used, Sybil, "interesting complications" – and he will ring back in an hour's time to tell you himself.'

'Such a fine man, that Dingle chap. You can always trust a Dingle.'

The dogs stretched and snuffled.

'Wait,' said Mrs Kavanagh. 'Rook is nearby. I sense him.'

They felt the fluttering of wings skim over their heads. The sleek black rook settled itself comfortably on Mrs Kavanagh's outstretched arm. The dogs did not budge.

'There you are, Rook. I knew you were listening. Pay close attention tonight, won't you?'

Rook turned his head towards Mrs Kavanagh, pecked gently at her shoulder and hopped onto her lap as Pilpenny turned the wheelchair back towards the bridge.

'Come on, lovies,' Mrs Kavanagh called to her dogs. 'Might as well all hear what Mr Dingle himself has to say, mmm?'

After Mrs Kavanagh had spoken with Mr Dingle, she said, 'That Mr Dingle has done a bang-up job! He's there, he is! I say, I haven't felt so cheery in a long time, Pilpenny, have you? Bring us some sherry, won't you? We'll celebrate.'

Mrs Kavanagh stretched her arm towards the window. Rook flew to her from his windowsill perch.

'And you, too, Rook. You, too, shall celebrate.'

CHAPTER 27

The Limits of Friendship

I'd spent all morning in the barn, clearing clutter from around Joe's workbench and organizing what was left. I didn't accomplish much in the first hour because I stopped to examine each thing: lengths of rope; balls of twine; jars of screws and nails and tacks; cans of paint, oil and turpentine; parts of engines; screwdrivers and hammers. The oddest things made me stop, reminding me of ways they had been used.

That near-empty green paint can: Joe had let me use that paint on an ancient bicycle I'd found in the barn. I liked that colour so much that I went on to paint one of his ladders, Nula's treasured milk can that she used as a flower container and half a barn door. Joe and Nula didn't look as pleased as I had expected. All Joe said was, 'I guess you like that green colour,' and Nula said, about her milk can, 'It's...very *green*, isn't it?'

A tangle of twine on Joe's workbench reminded me of a time when I was maybe five or six and had taken a ball of twine and wound it all through the chicken yard, so the chickens would have little 'rooms' of their own, and Nula came out in the near dark and tripped over the twine rooms and broke her wrist when she fell.

She didn't yell. She didn't scold. All she said to me was, 'Rooms for *chickens*?'

After the first hour of poking around in the barn, I snapped out of it and became ruthless. Nine empty cans? Don't need nine. Toss six. Six balls of twine? Toss three. Rusty nails? Toss 'em all. A growing pile of discards nearly blocked the barn door.

'Hey, tree girl.'

Finn's voice.

There he was, standing in the opening, with the morning light behind him, giving him a white-light halo all around his whole self. I didn't know how he got as far as the barn without the chickens raising a ruckus.

'I'm not "tree girl". I'm Naomi. *Nay-oh-me.* How come you remember Lizzie's name so well and can't remember mine?'

Finn smiled that slow, sweet smile of his. 'OK, Nay-oh-me, but remember that I'm Finn and not Finn boy.'

'OK.'

Finn bent to examine a tin can in the discard pile. 'You tossing these?'

'Yep. Got a million of them.'

'I could sure use a couple.'

'Help yourself.'

Finn picked up a discarded ball of twine. 'And this? Sure could use this.'

'It's all yours. What're you going to do with it?'

'Things. Stuff.' Finn inched closer. 'Looks like you're busy.'

'Me? Naw. Me?'

'Looks like you're clearing out this old barn.'

'Me?'

He came closer. 'Maybe you could use some help.'

'What, me?'

Finn was now standing directly in front of me. 'I like your face.'

'My face?'

'Naomi! Lar-de-dar! Naomi! You here? I've come to help!' And there was Lizzie Scatterdinghead, all clean and smiling, bopping along with the chickens squawking and pecking at her heels. 'Oh, it's Finn boy!' she squealed. 'What a surprise-a-dise! Lar-de-dar. Funny finding you here. Naomi and I were just talking about you yesterday, Finn boy. Naomi said you came over to see me on Sunday. Is that right, Finn boy? Why ever did you do that? What did you want? Hi, there, Naomi. You're all dirtied up, aren't you?'

How is it that you can be close friends with a person, deeply close friends, closer than sisters maybe, and then one day you want that person to disappear off the face of this earth? Sure, I've wanted to slip some tape on Lizzie's mouth a few dozen times, but I never before wanted her to vanish completely. That day in the barn, though, when my mouth was mere seconds from being magnetically drawn to Finn's mouth, and Lizzie burst through the door warbling *lar-de-dar*, I had a powerful wish for her to vanish in a puff of smoke.

I disliked her then. No, I *hated* her. I hated her clumsy babbling and her inability to *see* what a babbling idiot she could be. I hated that she thought she was so *nice* and so much a *friend*, when so many things she was doing seemed purposely aimed at making me miserable.

Finn's reaction to Lizzie's intrusion made me even more miserable. 'Hi there, Lizzie – or would you rather be called Elizabeth?'

'Why don't you call her "tree girl"?' I said.

Lizzie beamed. 'Finn boy, you can call me whatever you choose. I don't mind a bit what people call me, as long as it isn't mean or cruel. Most people call me Lizzie, only a few call me Elizabeth, one person I know calls me "tree girl" – ahem! – and my foster parents, who will soon be my real adoptive parents, sometimes they call me Elizabeth Niamh. Niamh is my middle name. You spell it n-i-a-m-h, but you say it like this: *NEE-av*—'

'You never told *me* that was your middle name,' I said.

'Why, Naomi, you never asked me! I don't even know *your* middle name, do I? And I don't know Finn's middle name, do I?'

'I like your voice,' Finn said.

He was talking to Lizzie. I wanted to choke her.

'My *voice*? What a wonderfully sweet thing for you to say. I think I must be blushing all over the place. Am I? Am I blushing?' She put her hands to her cheeks. 'Oh, I certainly *feel* warm, so I must be blushing. Naomi, rescue me, please! Finn boy, don't you like Naomi's voice, too? I think Naomi has a nice voice, a little low for a girl, but some people like those low voices better than my kind of voice.'

Lizzie went on like that for some time until Finn said he had to leave. 'Where do you have to go, Finn boy? Are you going back to the Dimmenses? Do you *like* staying up there on Black Dog Night Hill? Aren't you scared? Or are you going to Crazy Cora's? Or Witch Wiggins's place? You shouldn't go there. I don't understand why you go to such … such strange places with such strange occupants. Why do you do that, Finn boy?'

Finn seemed numbed by her questions. 'I don't know which of those questions I should answer first, so I won't answer any, if it's all right with you.' He smiled at me and at Lizzie and sauntered out of the barn door and out of sight.

'Well!' Lizzie said. 'He could have stayed to *help*! Honestly, boys will do *anything* to get out of work. I'll help you, though. What do you want me to do?'

That was a dangerous question. I wanted her to fall down dead of a heart attack. I wanted the chickens to peck a hole in her head. I wanted her to zing off to her precious moon and stay there.

'Lizzie, I'm awful tired. I've been at this all morning, and all I want to do is take a shower and a long nap.'

'Naomi, you poor thing. I understand completely. You stop working right this minute. Don't worry about me.'

'I won't, Lizzie. I won't worry about you.'

'Good!' As she started across the yard, chickens swarmed around her. 'Shoo, shoo, go on now, you silly chickens. Shoo, shoo.' She turned to wave at me. 'Maybe I'll try to catch up with Finn boy! Bye, Naomi, bye-bye!'

Oh. Yes, I *would* worry about Lizzie.

CHAPTER 28

Don't Get Too Friendly

Once when I was little, Joe found me cradling a chicken in my beloved, tattered blankie.

'Naomi, don't you get too friendly with that chicken.'

'Why not?'

'Not *too* friendly, not with chickens.'

'Why?'

'Because.'

A couple months later, I was on the back screened porch one drizzly morning, trying to see over the windowsill into the yard. Joe came out of the barn, snatched up a chicken – Miss Buddy – by the neck, slammed her on the old tree trunk, lifted his hatchet and chopped off her head. The headless Miss Buddy rolled off the stump and ran around the yard for several minutes before falling over.

'Dinner!' he called out to Nula at the kitchen window.

I guess you could say that left an impression on me.

Somehow in my mind that scene got mixed up with the dog attack and blood and my arm and my father's arm. One night I dreamed that the sheriff came to our house to arrest me and my father, and he took us over to the stump and told us to put our arms on it and he chopped them off. *Whack.*

I didn't trust people or animals very easily. Except for Finn. I hadn't known that boy one day before I had willingly given him a chunk of my young heart.

As for Lizzie, I hadn't trusted her when we first met, but she sort of wore me down. 'Naomi, please will you sit with me? You're the most clever girl I ever met. I wish I were half as clever as you' and, 'Naomi, I wish I could sit as still as you. You look as if you are watching a movie in your head. Are you? Tell me about it! Will you?' and, 'Naomi, how do you remember everyone's name? How do you *do* that? Names jump in and out of my head like grasshoppers.'

But after that morning in the barn with Finn, I started to wonder if maybe I shouldn't be so friendly with Lizzie. What if she really *wasn't* my friend?

I took a shower and lay down on my bed and closed my eyes. My body felt heavy, as if it might sink into the mattress and into a deep, deep sleep. I could see Finn's face coming closer and closer to mine.

'Naomi?'

'What? What?'

'Easy, lass, it's only me.' Nula stood at the foot of my bed.

An enormous sigh escaped out into the air. I couldn't help it.

'What is it, Naomi?'

'It's that Finn boy.' Another sigh of great depth. 'I feel as if I'm either going to die or sprout wings and flap around the yard.'

Nula placed her fingertips against my forehead. 'Why, lass, you're heartsick, that's what. You drink some hot tea with a dollop of honey in it, and then go out and run fast and hard.'

'Sounds like the cure for an ailing donkey.'

'Sometimes there's not much difference between a heartsick soul and a sick ole donkey.' She tapped my foot. 'Have you seen that Finn boy again?'

'He was here this morning. In the barn.'

'Was he? I heard Lizzie crashing through the yard, but I missed dreamy Finn boy. Shoot. I was hoping to get a look at him.'

I ran across the meadow and down the hill. I ran alongside the creek, and with every step, I was thinking, *Finn, Finn, Finn, Finn.* Where the creek turned, I stopped. There he was: Finn. Maybe I could summon him just by thinking about him.

'You looking for me?' he asked.

I was panting like an old dog. I couldn't speak.

Finn walked towards me. He *glided* towards me. He *floated* towards me. I felt I would faint. I was hallucinating.

'Naomi?'

I collapsed in a heap on the bank. 'Whoa. A little dizzy, that's all.'

Finn knelt beside me. His hand touched my cheek. It felt like silky air whispering across my face. 'Naomi?'

'Mmm?'

His lips touched my cheek, lightly, like the swish of a butterfly's wing, and because I felt awkward and did not know how to respond, I lifted his hand and softly kissed his palm.

The next morning, as I was on my way to meet Lizzie and Mrs Mudkin to save some more unfortunate souls, I replayed my encounter with Finn. I wanted to remember everything so that I would be able to see it in my mind so perfectly, so accurately that it would be as if it were happening again.

I had asked Finn to tell me where he was from and why he was here, but he said, 'I'd rather hear about you. Tell me where *you're* from and why *you're* here and what you like and what you don't, and—'

'That's not interesting to me.'

'But it's interesting to me.' He wasn't shy about saying it. He said it casually, sincere but not mushy.

We had moved up the bank and were sitting with our backs against a boulder. The creek was shiny with the afternoon sun overhead, shooting speckled arrows at us. Flickers of light and shadow played across Finn's face.

I truly did not want to talk about myself. Mine is not a story that can be repeated too often. Not only did it seem too heavy to drag out, but I felt as if I did not have all the pieces of it, that I would not be able to tell my story until I was an old lady.

Finn asked about my parents. I told him – in the briefest and simplest way – about my mother dying when I was a baby, and about my father and the dog and all that.

'That's tragic,' he said. 'Is that why your arm is like that?'

I stiffened. 'Like what?'

'Like it got hurt real bad.'

I never talked about my arm, unless I had to defend it against the likes of Bo Dimmens and his idiot insults. Most other people around here knew what happened to me and they knew my right arm got torn up pretty bad, but they didn't point it out to me. Maybe that arm would never be strong and would never grow straight like the other one, but that didn't seem too bad in the scheme of things.

CHAPTER 29

Reluctant Souls

I was dreading the encounter with the next two unfortunate souls because they were Witch Wiggins and Crazy Cora, but I was also curious about them. How scary could they really be? What would their houses look like? Did Witch Wiggins truly have coffins and a thousand birds? Finn had been there. Maybe Witch Wiggins would tell me something about Finn.

I had similar mixed feelings about seeing Lizzie again. I was annoyed with her, mad at her, but I also wanted to know if she had seen Finn. I wanted to tell her about my encounter with him so that she would understand that he was *my* Finn, mine. It sounds silly now to say that, but that's the way it was.

An orange scarf was wrapped around Lizzie's neck. 'Naomi,' she rasped, 'I have the worst sore throat. I almost have laryngitis.'

Shoot. She wouldn't be able to yammer at me all day long.

Mrs Mudkin insisted that Lizzie go home. 'You mustn't be exposing these elderly unfortunate souls to your germs. Off with you now. Go, go—'

I tried to protest. Worse than Lizzie yammering at me all day long would be me on my own with Mrs Mudkin and the unfortunate souls.

Lizzie waved a weak goodbye, her other hand clutching her throat in a gesture of dire agony.

'Come along,' Mrs Mudkin urged, tugging at my wrist. 'Unfortunate souls awaiting.'

We stood a long time on Witch Wiggins's porch, alternately knocking and calling out her name, not *Witch Wiggins*, of course, but *Mrs Wiggins*. From within came a low, whirring sound as of a thousand, thousand birds flapping their wings. Finally, a loud click and a thud and the door inched open and one eyeball appeared above the chain, which still held the door fastened.

When Mrs Mudkin explained our mission, Witch Wiggins replied with one word. 'No.'

'No?' Mrs Mudkin said. 'No what?'

'No, I'm not here and I don't want any and I don't need any.'

Mrs Mudkin smiled. 'Now, now, surely the company of this – this – young lady will be a welcome pleasure in your day.' Mrs Mudkin beamed at me and then turned again to the eye at the door frame.

'I'm in the middle of something,' Witch Wiggins said, closing the door and relatching three locks from the inside.

'Well!' Mrs Mudkin said. 'The manners of some people! Even if one is unfortunate and elderly it does not excuse one from common courtesy.' Abruptly, she turned and again yanked me by the wrist. 'We will try her next week. We will not be daunted. This way, Raynee—'

'Naomi. *Nay-OH-me.*'

'Raomi.'

'NAY. NAY. Like a horse: *neigh, neigh, neigh.*'

'Shh, child, don't be so silly.'

When we reached Crazy Cora's house, we encountered an unshaven man in overalls sitting on the porch steps. Across his knees lay a rifle.

'Don't think you should come up no closer,' he said.

We stopped in our tracks.

'I beg your pardon?' Mrs Mudkin said in her sweetest voice.

'Maw don't want no trespassers.'

'Is Cora your maw – your mother – young man?'

He wasn't a young man by any means, but he was younger than Mrs Mudkin. 'What's it to you?'

'Young man, I am Mrs Mudkin from the Ladies Society at the church and I am here with this young lady, Raomi, to assist your mother.'

'She knows you were coming and she said to tell you she don't need no assistance.'

Mrs Mudkin rearranged her hat so that two feathers stuck out straight from the right side of her head. 'Young man, I think I would prefer to hear that directly from Cora.'

The man turned his head towards the house and bellowed,

'MAW! THIS HERE LADY WANTS TO HEAR IT FROM YOU DIRE-ECK-LY.'

A face appeared at an upstairs window: a white face surrounded by a tangle of white hair. The voice of Crazy Cora drifted down. 'I don't need no assistance. I am taking a nap.'

The face withdrew from the window. The man smiled at us.

'See?' he said. 'I told ya.'

I hate to admit it, but I was happy that Crazy Cora and Witch Wiggins did not require my help that day. I raced home feeling as if I'd been given a gift: a free day. A free day always felt better when you hadn't expected it to be free. Free!

I planned to let Nula know I'd been set free and then I'd roam. I'd wander here and there, free of Lizzie and hoping to bump into Finn, my Finn.

As I rounded the final curve leading to our house, I saw a lump up ahead at the side of the road. At first it looked like a sack of garbage, but the closer I got, the less it looked like garbage and the more it looked like a person. Every now and then, but not too often, you might run into a drunk lying alongside the road. Normally, you steered clear of them, but this one was lying between me and our gate.

And then I saw that it was not a drunk. It was Joe. I lurched towards him and then stopped. There was blood near his head and his right arm. I started screaming like a crazy person, screaming a sound I had never heard come out of my mouth before, wailing and yelping and calling for help. I found out later that I was also screaming, 'Dog, dog! A dog has gotten Joe! Help! A dog!'

Nula came rushing from the house carrying a broom, looking wildly around for this dog. Then she saw Joe. She was at his side, her face down low next to his.

'Naomi, stop screaming. There's no dog. Run get help. Run like you've never run before.'

I did. I ran like I'd never run before, and that was the first time since I'd met Finn that I did not think of him, not once.

CHAPTER 30

Across The Ocean: Another Call

MRS KAVANAGH

Across the ocean, it was a chilly July afternoon, but all the windows were open, at the request of Mrs Kavanagh.

'Fresh air, clean air, new air!' she commanded. 'Let's pull down those heavy curtains, Pilpenny. Full of dust, don't you think?' From her wheelchair, Mrs Kavanagh tugged at a thick, brocaded curtain.

Pilpenny said, 'It's easy enough for you to say, "Let's" as if you mean, "Let us" – the *two* of us – do the work, but you really mean me, don't you, Sybil, mmm? Let ole Pilpenny do all the work. Pilpenny the slave!'

'Now, Pilpenny, *tuh*! You silly hen. Don't throw a wobbly. Listen – there's the phone. See who's ringing us up, won't you, Pilpenny, sweet?'

'Sweet *slave*. Sometimes I'm sorry Mr Dingle introduced us.' Pilpenny tapped the top of Mrs Kavanagh's head and scuttled off to the hall. When she returned, she said, 'Sybil, it's the Dingle man.'

'What does he want?'

'You'd best come to the phone.' Pilpenny wheeled Mrs Kavanagh into the hall and stood discreetly to one side as Mrs Kavanagh took the phone.

'Dingle?' she said. 'Again so soon? What is it? Eh? Say again? My, my, my. Yes, I see. Yes, please do. My, my.'

After ending her call, Mrs Kavanagh turned to Pilpenny. 'This *does* put a wrinkle in things, doesn't it?'

CHAPTER 31

Wrinkles

The next week was a fog of days and nights, dripping with muffled weeping and visitors coming and going, and the same questions asked and answered:

'A heart attack, was it?'

'Yes.'

'Just like that?'

'Yes.'

'No warning?'

'No.'

The first time Nula was asked whether Joe had had any warning, she hesitated. The only thing out of the ordinary that morning had been his saying his hand itched. He'd held out his hand, palm up, and said, 'Itches like crazy. What's that mean?'

Nula said, 'It means company's coming.'

'Shoot,' Joe said. 'Don't want no company!'

All week long, similar phrases salted the air:

'At least he went quickly.'

'He was a good man.'

'He'll be in heaven now.'

'He was a nice man.'

'He was an honest fellow.'

And there were the odd recollections, offered in earnest:

'Once't he saved my donkey, didja know that?'

'We caught frogs together when we was kids.'

'Once't he was sweet on my cousin Irene.'

'Once't he stole a watermelon. His daddy whupped him for it.'

When people asked Nula, 'What will you do now?' she looked back at them blankly, as if they had said, 'Are you a rhinoceros?'

On the day of the funeral, I found her standing in the dining room, tugging at the tablecloth. She was more agitated than I'd ever seen her. She pounded on the table, tugged at the cloth.

'This…this…tablecloth! Look at it – full of…of… wrinkles!' She slumped into a nearby chair and sobbed as if her heart were splattering into a zillion pieces.

I leaned my head against her back and spoke into that splattered heart. 'It's OK, Nula. I'll iron it. I'll get rid of the wrinkles.'

Outside, a man stood near the front gate, turning his hat in his hand, as if debating whether or not to approach our door. It was that Dingle Dangle man. He was gone by the time we left for the church.

I think Nula was surprised that I made it through the funeral, given that I'd spent the first twenty-four hours after Joe died in a stupor: unable to eat or sleep or move. The doctor later said my mind must have connected seeing Joe lying there – bleeding from cuts to his head and arm from when he fell – with the old memories of the dog attack and seeing my father lying on the grass, bloodied.

During those hours, I felt as if I'd twice lost a father – one young and one old. Something had shifted profoundly, as if a mountain had risen where flat earth had been, as if the blue sky had fallen away like a curtain, revealing a sombre, grey, domed lid.

But within a few days, there was another shift. I could hear Joe's voice; I could see him in my mind's eye – in the barn, in the fields, in the kitchen; I could sense him nearby. Not only could I hear him, see him and sense him, but it seemed perfectly natural that this was so. I soon learned, though, that not everyone shared this vision.

After the funeral service, the parlour and the dining room were crowded with townspeople and with food brought by the church ladies. I thought I would scream from hearing the same things over and over, about how sorry everyone was and yet what a 'blessing' it was that Joe had gone quickly. I knew they meant well, but I wanted to stand on the table and shout, 'Shut UP. Stop it! He's not gone. Go home.'

And then there was Lizzie. She had come to the house several times in the days before the funeral, but each time I'd been in bed and didn't want to see her. But now I was trapped in a chair in the corner.

Her face crumpled when she spotted me and tears dribbled down her cheeks.

'Naomi, Naomi, baby, you poor thing, you poor little thing.'

I do not know what came over me. I pushed at her and said, 'I'm not a baby. I'm not a poor little thing, Lizzie.' I couldn't bear that she was going to start saying Joe was gone.

She sniffled, taken aback. 'Naomi?'

I glanced round the room. 'Where's Finn? I thought surely you and he would be hanging out together by now.'

'What are you talking about?'

I don't know how the funeral and jealousy were related, but that day the two were joined at the hip. 'You know what I'm talking about, Lizzie. Don't act so innocent. You've been after

Finn since the first day you met him.'

Lizzie took two steps back. 'Let me get somebody—' Her eyes searched the crowd.

'I don't need anybody, and I especially don't need you.' I got up and pushed past her and made my way out into the yard. The chickens were penned up. Feeble attempts had been made to rake the yard where they usually strutted.

'Hey.' A boy's voice came from the side of the house. 'Hey.' It was Bo Dimmens. He was a big lug of a boy, awkwardly stuffed into a too-small suit.

I glared at him. I didn't feel any obligation to be polite to Bo Dimmens, given the misery he had caused me over the years.

'Sorry,' he said.

'Sorry about what?'

'About, you know – Joe.'

'Why are you sorry about Joe?'

His upper lip curled and he snorted like an old hog. He didn't reply.

'Where's that Finn boy?' I asked.

Bo snorted again. 'Who?'

'You know who. That Finn boy who's been staying up at your place with all your-your-people and all those-those-dogs.'

Bo looked at the sky, at the ground and back at the house. I thought he might be checking for witnesses to the punch he was about to launch at me. He put his hands in his pockets. 'I don't know what you are babbling about, girl. I don't know why I came here anyways. Joe shot my dog.'

'What? Are you crazy out of your mind?'

'He shot my dog. Ever'body knows that.'

'Well, I don't know it, and I'm part of "ever'body", aren't I?'

'Then you're plain ignorant.'

'Me? You're calling *me* ignorant? Am I the one who flunked two grades in school?'

He reached down and scooped up a clod of dirt. 'Not ever'body has the same advantages as you.'

Advantages might be the longest word I ever heard fall out of Bo Dimmens's mouth.

'What are you talking about? You're standing there like a big meat carcass telling *me* I've had more advantages than *you*? *Me?* The one with no mother and no daddy and a wobbled-up arm and…and…everybody saying Joe is gone? You see those things as advantages, Bo Dimmens?'

The clod of dirt in Bo's hands crumbled as he squeezed it. Bits dropped to the ground.

'Well, I might have to think about that some more. I was thinking you had some learnin' advantages, but now I don't know. If you don't even know about Joe shootin' my dog, then you probably don't know a lot of things.'

I picked up my own clod of dirt. 'I do so. Like what?'

'Like I bet you don't even know why nobody in this little lick town has a dog.' He laughed, bits of spit splattering the air. 'Ha, I can tell by the look on your face that it never even occurred to your pea brain – you prob'ly never even noticed that nobody has a dog.'

I longed to fly to the moon. I longed to be far, far away.

'I thought so,' Bo said. 'Now who's the ignorant one? You don't even know it was my dog that et up your arm and your daddy. You don't even know that you was so stupid as to whack that dog with a stick in the first place. You don't even know that Joe shot my dog. You don't even know that Joe went round to every house in this town and convinced people what a danger dogs were. You don't even know that's why *we* ended up with ever'body's dogs. You don't know nothin', do you? I feel sorry for you, girl, cuz you're as ignorant as that there dirt clod you're holdin'.'

I threw it at him. I picked up another and threw it, too, glad that the dirt clung to his suit. 'You get out of here, Bo Dimmens. You get out of here right now.'

'Don't mind if I do,' he said, and he ambled down the drive as casually as if he were taking a Sunday stroll.

Inside, I bumped straight into a clump of unfortunate souls snatching cookies from the kitchen counter: Mr Canner, one-armed Farley, Crazy Cora and Witch Wiggins. The men wore wrinkled suits, Crazy Cora was wrapped in a blue satin robe and Witch Wiggins looked completely terrifying in a long, black dress.

They were chattering and clucking like chickens.

'I'll have one of those red cherry ones.'

'Pistachio, pistachio!'

'Those aren't pistachios.'

'These are too crumbly.'

'Those hurt my teeth.'

Then they spotted me.

Crazy Cora said, 'You was at my house with that Mudflap lady, wasn't you?'

Witch Wiggins corrected her. 'Not Mud*flap*, it's Mud*top*. They tried to get into my house, too.'

'And mine,' Mr Canner said. 'Threw out all my mail.'

'Tried to make me go for a walk,' Mr Farley added.

'Joe stole my dog, you know,' Crazy Cora said to no one in particular. Then she turned to me. 'Joe stole my dog. Hers, too.' She pointed to Witch Wiggins.

'Took 'em in the dead of night. Said they was kid-eaters.'

By this time, they were inching towards me like a pack of hungry wolves, and I was backed up against the door.

Crazy Cora waved a cookie at me. 'Believed him at the time.'

'Felt sorry for him,' Witch Wiggins said.

One-armed Farley said, 'Enough to make a grown man cry, what with all that blood and wailing going on.'

Mr Canner was holding on to the back of a chair for support. He closed his eyes. 'I don't want to think about it. It was awful.'

The long, thin hand on the long, thin arm of Witch Wiggins reached towards me and smoothed my hair. 'But *you* were there, *you* know.'

I stared at each of those faces. Had they all seen it? Had the whole town seen it?

'But I *don't* know,' I whispered, backing out of the room.

CHAPTER 32

A Patch of Dirt

Where I wanted to go was the moon, as far, as far away as I could go. There I would not be able to hear chatter about blood and death. There I would be able to see all the larger world beyond our place, beyond Blackbird Tree, beyond our whole country, beyond our earth.

I fled to the barn and clambered up into the loft. The late-afternoon sun streaked through cracks between the boards, filling the loft with stripes of thick, dancing dust. A layer of hay covered the floor. A mouse dashed across a rafter.

Old egg crates were sloppily stacked along one side of the loft, a pile of ropes and rags slumped near the window and on the far wall loomed the trunks. They were large, sturdy wooden trunks with heavy brass hinges and locks. When I used to play up here, I rode the rounded-top one like a horse. The two flat-topped ones were, variously, food wagons, hay wagons, train cars, houses, even islands. I'd never seen the contents of the trunks, but according to Joe and Nula, one contained my father's things, one my mother's and one Nula's.

When I'd asked Joe why he and I didn't have trunks, he replied, 'We don't have any junk worth saving, Naomi.'

I probably assumed the trunks were full of old clothes and blankets, nothing of interest to me. Until, that is, the day I heard Joe say to Nula, 'When are you going to get rid of those trunks?'

'Why, I can't do that,' she said.

'Don't see why not. They're just full of dead ... things.'

'They are *not* dead. You leave those trunks alone, Joe.'

And somehow, my young mind took that to mean there was something *living* in the trunks. That night I dreamed it was my parents in the trunks, shrunken and clawing to get out. They called to me, 'Naomi, Naomi, let us out—'

Nula tried to comfort me. 'Shh, shh,' she said. 'Just by living, just by being Naomi, you are letting them out.'

Although I did not know what she meant, it must have reassured me that night, but I avoided the trunks from that day on.

Now, in the loft, fleeing the funeral crowd, I heard, 'Naomi.' The voice was soft, whispered. 'Naomi.'

I stepped away from the trunks.

'Naomi, it's me.'

There was Finn, at the loft ladder.

'You scared me,' I said. 'I didn't hear you.'

'You never hear me ... until I'm here.'

I was happy to see Finn, but I felt awkward, so troubled by the day and the talk of dogs and of Joe.

'What's in those?' Finn asked, gesturing towards the trunks.

'Stuff.'

Finn looked different, but I wasn't sure how exactly. He wasn't dressed up like everyone else, and there was dust in his hair, as if he'd been sleeping in the loft. He moved to the round-topped trunk, Nula's. 'This one's really old, isn't it? Now, *that's* the one I'd like to open.'

'Naomi, Naomi!' It was Nula, calling from the yard

I went to the loft window. 'Up here, Nula.'

She cocked her head, crossed her arms and stared up at me for a good long minute. She glanced back at the house and then up at the barn loft again. 'I'd be up there, too, if I could. Anyone up there with you?'

'No.'

'Come on down soon, you hear?'

'I will.'

Nula had not been back to Ireland since she came to America when she was twelve. She did not often talk about her family, but this much I knew: that she didn't think any of her six siblings were still alive and that her parents were long since dead. Sometimes she sang fragments of songs from when she was young; sometimes she told stories of a boy she had adored, but always these stories ended abruptly with, 'Ach, the boy who broke hearts, may you never meet such a lad, Naomi.'

But neither Nula nor Joe were dwellers in the past. Joe's youth must have been hard, too, for he would say, 'Then was then, and now is now, and why would I want to bring back that hardscrabble life and always a hungry belly?' Nula would add, 'Aye, aye, and the cold hands and the cold feet and the crying in the night.'

After Joe's funeral and after the last of the visitors had left the house, Nula sat on the back porch, looking out across the fields. When I asked what she was thinking, she said, 'Ah, Naomi, ah. I am thinking about all the years Joe and I worked together and how much time and energy and effort we put in – ah, never mind – it all-it all-goes away.' She waved her hand in front of her as if she were scattering seed to the wind. 'Nothing left but a patch of dirt and a crooked house.'

CHAPTER 33

Across the Ocean: A Visitor Returns

Mrs Kavanagh

'He's here, Sybil, your Dingle fellow. I'll show him in and leave you two alone.' Pilpenny wheeled Mrs Kavanagh closer to the fireplace and kneeled to stoke the logs. The day had been balmy, but once the sun had set, a chill descended on the massive stone house.

'Pilpenny, I'd rather you stay. We will need your help. And please bring my two lovies.'

Mrs Kavanagh had not slept well the past few nights, and the fatigue lay heavily on her shoulders. She wore a long, deep blue dress of the finest wool, matching heels that were sensible yet stylish, a long string of pearls and a finely wrought gold bracelet with a single charm attached. Her hair was true silver, neither grey nor white, and gathered in soft puffs around her face.

'Ah, Sybil!' Mr Dingle said, bowing elegantly before Mrs Kavanagh. 'You are always the epitome of refinement.'

'Is that so? It is you, Dingle, whom I think of as the epitome of refinement. Not me, with my coarse upbringing, surely.'

'One can always polish coarseness, as you so well have shown, Sybil.'

Mr Dingle seated himself across from Mrs Kavanagh. Pilpenny pulled a chair to one side of Mrs Kavanagh, and the elegant white foxhounds, Sadie and Maddie, folded themselves at their owner's feet.

'Now, Dingle, let's get right down to business. Is the plan in jeopardy? I haven't slept a wink since you phoned from America. Thank you for coming directly back.'

'I'm so sorry, Sybil, that you have been troubled. I have done some further thinking and perhaps what I have to tell you will be reassuring. Let me fill you in on what I have learned. There is much to tell, but first I must tell you this: the girls talked of a boy named Finn.'

Mrs Kavanagh leaned forward. 'What did you say? Finn?'

'Yes, Finn.'

'How odd. Odd, but . . . somehow . . . perfect. Don't you think that's perfect, Pilpenny?'

Pilpenny put her hand to her throat. 'Mmm.'

The dogs stretched and yawned and rolled onto their sides.

'Everything is pretty much in place, Sybil. Joe's dying was sad, of course, but in the end, it makes things easier.'

'Brilliant,' Mrs Kavanagh said. 'Absolutely brilliant!' She lifted her arm, beckoning the rook. 'Rook, listen to this.'

CHAPTER 34

Two Trunks

The next morning, I felt as if I'd been trampled by a herd of cows. Outside, Nula was standing in the yard, surrounded by clucking chickens. Miss Johnny was having a fit. *Ooka, ooka, ooka! Ooka!* Nula held a feed bucket in one hand. Her other hand was suspended in midair.

'Nula?'

She turned slowly, as if in a trance.

I took the bucket and scattered feed to the chickens.

Nula flailed her arms at them. 'These-these silly chickens! Stop that stupid clucking!'

'Nula?'

'Everything's so-so messy.' She turned this way and that. 'So very messy. We'll have to sell the place. We'll have to move.'

I watched the chickens scurrying and pecking, oblivious to us.

The following day, Lizzie appeared at our door after breakfast.
Her eyelids were swollen, her face puffy and pale.

'Naomi, Naomi, it's the most awful thing. I have to talk to
you or I will die. I'm not wanted.' Lizzie sobbed on my shoulder.
'Not wanted!'

'Don't be so dramatic. Of course you're wanted.'

'No, listen, it's truly tragic.' She sniffed and choked on her
sobs. 'The Cupwrights ... the Cupwrights—'

'Spit it out, Lizzie.'

'The Cupwrights simply do not want me. They are not
going to adopt me.' Loud wailing followed.

'How do you know that?'

'They told me, Naomi. They told me! I don't think I will
live!' She sobbed loud, gulping sobs.

Nula found me and Lizzie in the loft, our backs against the
trunks, lost in thought.

'Girls, you need to move. We're going to deal with these
trunks today. Sit up! Step back! We may have some ghosts flying
around here.'

I think I may have whimpered. 'Now? Why *now*?'

'Because it's about time,' Nula said. Something had come
over her; she was determined. 'It will be good for us. Which one
first, Naomi? You choose.'

We started with my father's trunk, which took a key, hammer and screwdriver to open. On top were several issues of *The Ravensworth Times*. The newspapers contained, in succession, these headlines:

DOG ATTACKS CHILD

BLACKBIRD TREE MAN SAVES DAUGHTER FROM VICIOUS DOG

CHILD IN CRITICAL CONDITION FROM DOG ATTACK

BLACKBIRD TREE MAN DIES FROM DOG ATTACK

VICIOUS DOG SHOT

'Gosh,' Lizzie said, 'these are purely terrifying. Look at these pictures—'

There were only two photos: one of my father in the hospital, wrapped in gauze from head to foot, and one of me in the hospital, my head looking so small against a pillow, my arm and leg bandaged. I could not connect that that was my face. That Naomi looked so frightened and lost.

'I don't want to read these,' I said.

'Should we toss them?' Nula asked.

'Yes.' My answer came so quickly it surprised me. I felt as if that father and that little girl had been stuffed in a trunk far too long.

Nula put the papers to one side and retrieved a box of photographs. I lifted the lid, feeling as if I were prying. Who were these people? Was that my father? Was that another Naomi? That woman with him – I knew she was my mother, but I did not feel any connection with these people.

A uniform, boots and a dog tag told me that my father had been in the army. *Should I have known this?* Two musty high school yearbooks lay on the bottom of the trunk. We found photos of him in each. He'd played basketball and baseball. That father might be disappointed to see that I would never play either one of those sports well.

And all the while, I felt relieved that Joe had not left a trunk. I didn't need dead trunk things. If I closed my eyes, I would see Joe down below at his workbench. I would hear him tapping a screwdriver against a can.

Nula set aside items to be thrown away or donated and began returning the rest to the trunk. As Lizzie was stacking the newspapers, she put her hand out to us and said, 'What? Is this—? What? Look at this! I can hardly believe—'

She was looking at the photograph again, the one of me in the hospital bed.

'Lizzie, I said I don't want those.'

'Yes, you do. You won't believe' – she flapped the paper in front of my face – 'this! Look here.'

'What?' I said, annoyed. 'I've seen it already.'

'No, *here*,' she said, tapping the photo of me, bandaged, in the bed. 'Who is *this*?'

'For heaven's sake, Lizzie. It's that other Naomi.'

Nula was now studying the photo. 'You mean the nurse?'

I hadn't even noticed the nurse standing beside the bed.

'Yes!' Lizzie said. Her face was flushed, her hands trembling. 'This is not just any nurse. This is my *mother*. My very own *mother*. Look at this, Naomi. You met her. She probably saved your life! I knew we were connected. I knew it.'

Lizzie pressed the photo to her, released it, studied it, kissed the photo and pressed it to her again. 'May I keep this, oh, please, may I?'

Both Nula and I were stunned into silence.

'I just cannot believe this, Naomi. It's like, it's like – the universe spun us together on purpose.'

'Yes,' Nula said quietly. 'It does seem that way, doesn't it?'

What was Nula thinking? Was she wondering why the universe had spun Joe out of her life? Or why I was spun into her life?

While Lizzie clung to the newspaper, Nula turned to my mother's trunk. She said, 'I have no idea what's in here.' With a turn of the key, the lid popped open. 'I wish I'd known your mother, Naomi.' To Lizzie, Nula added, 'Naomi and her father moved here when Naomi was nearly one.'

I wondered where we'd lived before that.

A pink, blank baby book rested on top; beneath that was a packet of cards in a rubber band that split when I removed it:

CONGRATULATIONS! IT'S A GIRL!
AN ANGEL FOR YOU!
BABY CONGRATULATIONS!
WELCOME, BABY!

I was so disoriented that I said, 'What were these for?'

Lizzie and Nula exchanged a look. Lizzie said, 'Naomi, you idjit, they were probably for you!'

My mother's trunk was stuffed with photos and cards and items of clothing: a lavender prom dress, cowboy boots, a sparkly skirt. As I removed each item, Lizzie reacted as if this were Christmas bounty.

'Look at *that*!' and 'Ohhhh!' and 'Naomi, look!'

I felt removed, unable to share her excitement. It was as if there remained some of that old, childish worry – that there was something living buried in the trunk, or that something else unexpected and unpleasant would emerge.

Slowly I pulled out a wooden box with a heart painted on it, a musty book about horses, a box of shells and a drawing of a river with trees along the bank.

Lizzie was enchanted. 'Oh! Naomi! Oh!' and 'You should keep this, Naomi!' and 'How perfectly perfect!' She pressed the book to her chest, cradled the shells in her hands and traced the drawing with one finger. You would have thought it was her own mother's things we were examining.

Nula sat to one side, stacking everything in a neat pile.

What is the matter with me? I thought I should feel as Lizzie did, or at least be able to *recognize* something. I thought I should be able to say, *This was my mother's*, to say it with authority. But I could not.

Lizzie examined a tattered notebook. 'Look here, Naomi, this must be your mother's handwriting.' She held the book open to a page marked 'Learn these!' Below was a list of biological terms I did not recognize. In the margins was my mother's name written several ways:

Kathleen King
Kathleen Deane
Kathleen M. Deane
Kathleen King Deane
Mr Kathleen Deane
Mr Andrew Deane

I'd known my mother's name was Kathleen, but I hadn't known her maiden name or her middle name. *A person ought to know her mother's whole name*, I thought.

'What does the *M* stand for? What was her middle name?'

'No idea,' Nula said.

We decided to toss some of the more faded, cheap clothing and all of the magazines. I skimmed a few of the cards before tossing them on the discard pile. I recognized none of the names: Franny and Maggie, and Phyllis and Jeannie, Freddy and Mick. Mr and Mrs Loughlin. Mrs Kindrick. Several were from someone named Artie, who always added a heart after his name, which seemed a strange thing for a male to do.

The rest we returned to the trunk.

As we were about to open Nula's trunk, Lizzie blurted out to Nula, 'The Cupwrights don't want me. They're not going to adopt me.'

'What's that? Now, now, I'm sure they will—'

'No! They *told* me. Yesterday. They *told* me they were not going to adopt me. Well, what they said was that they *couldn't*, but I didn't even listen about why not because I knew what they meant. I knew exactly that they did not want me, they've never wanted me and they never will, and I could just die.'

'Now, now, Lizzie—'

'I am in their way. I cost too much to feed. I don't eat all *that* much, although I do regret having four slices of toast the other day because that probably looked exceedingly greedy, oh, where will I end up? Will I be sleeping in a cardboard box behind Tebop's store? Will I—'

'Shh,' Nula said. 'Don't you worry. Something will work out. Aren't there any other relatives of your own parents you could go to?'

'No. Nobody, not a single soul, except for some crazy old aunt in England, or maybe it's Scotland, or maybe it's Ireland, and I surely would rather sleep in a cardboard box than go a million miles away to live with a crazy aunt.'

'Do you know anything about her? Maybe she's not crazy at all.'

Lizzie looked offended. 'I'm certain she is crazy. My mother told me so, and it was her own sister, and as for her name, it is something completely ridiculous, like Hillbunny or Pushbunny, or something like that. Oh, what am I going to *do*?'

I once heard someone ask Nula how she went on after I dropped into their lives. Nula replied, 'You get up and you go on.' Thinking that I should offer some wisdom to Lizzie, I said,

'Lizzie, you just get up and then you go on,' but she did not receive this advice well.

'Easy for you to say, Naomi! Easy for *you*.'

~

'This trunk of mine,' Nula said as she wrestled with the lock of the third trunk, 'came with me on the ship when I sailed from Ireland. It belonged to an old man, a neighbour, who had taken pity on me when my family – thanks to the interference of that Finn boy—'

'Finn boy?' Lizzie said. 'What Finn boy?'

'Nula knew a boy named Finn when she was young.'

'Anyway, because of the interference of that Finn boy, my family handed me over to a shady-looking Irishman and his shady-looking wife, who had essentially bought me. I was to accompany them to America, where I would be working for a grand family, or so they said. I was twelve years old.'

'*Bought* you?' I said.

'Yes. They paid Finn – *Finn!* – a finder's fee, and they paid my parents a small sum and said that they were giving me the privilege of a new life in America and that the cost of my passage to America would be deducted from my first year's wages. They did not clarify that the cost of my passage would be deducted from *my whole year's wages*.'

'You worked for a year and earned nothing, is that what you mean?'

'Yes, Naomi. That's what I mean. And I did not work for a

"grand family"; I worked for the shady Irishman and his shady wife and their slovenly children. I worked from four in the morning until eleven at night, seven days a week, every day of the year.'

Lizzie said, 'But that's truly terrible. However did you survive?'

As the lid to the trunk popped open, issuing a puff of musty, trapped air, Nula said, 'You get up and then you go on.'

CHAPTER 35

Across The Ocean: Plans

MRS KAVANAGH

Mrs Kavanagh and Pilpenny were seated at one end of the long mahogany dining table. Sybil was telling Pilpenny about how she first came to Rooks Orchard.

'. . . And so Paddy, who wasn't called Paddy then – all full of sweet talk and flowers and promises – he finds a job for me as cook's helper here at Rooks Orchard. And what does he do? He collects my first month's wages, tells the Mistress that he will give them to me and then he does a runner, with my wages in his pocket. That wretched Paddy McCoul.'

'The warthog.'

'For years and years, I thought he'd run off to America, following my sister.'

'He didn't, though.'

'No, he didn't.'

'And what was it like for you here, with your *brekkinhart'* –
Pilpenny tapped her own heart – 'pining away for the wretched
warthog?'

'There I was, the poor cook's girl, knowing only how to peel
potatoes and empty slop buckets and feed hogs, and with my
heart broken. Nothing quite so pitiful as a young girl with a
broken heart, is there, Pilpenny?'

'Mmm.'

'You think you will not live, that you cannot go on.'

'Mmm.'

'But I was a hard worker, I was. I didn't see much of the
Master and the Mistress, but what I saw was enough to make
me shiver in my shoes, for they were stern and stiff as fence
posts and never a kind word to any of the help, only 'Fetch this'
and 'Fetch that' and 'Must you make so much noise?' and never
a thank you and never a look-you-in-the-eye.'

'Yes, that's what I've heard – that they were as cold as a
witch's toes.'

'Colder.'

'But Albert? He was not like them?'

'Ah, Albert, their only child. He was sixteen when I came
here. His mother called him her "frail one", and his father thought
him "as useless as a runt pig". And this because Albert was
quiet and kind and sensitive, fond of drawing and lying in the
grass.'

'Ah, Albert.'

'Sometimes when I'd be outside in the kitchen garden or on
my way to the hogs, I'd come across Albert, and naturally we

would talk from time to time. I remember one day early on when he and I were standing outside the kitchen door and his mother called from an upstairs window. She said, "Albert! What are you *doing*?" She said that as if he'd been caught standing in the hog pen with mud up to the knees of his fine trousers.'

'Ach!'

'And Albert's father – the Master – he whipped me with a switch from the apple tree. Many a time there was that I was whipped by the Master.'

'For shame!'

'So you can imagine how they reacted when we ran off together and married, eh? *Mercy!* The earth shook and the heavens yowled.'

'I'm surprised you ever came back here, Sybil.'

'I didn't want to, did I? But then the place came to Albert after his parents passed on, and sweet Albert, he merely wanted to stroll in the orchard and lie in the grass – and now, alas, he lies there permanently.'

'Poor Albert.'

'Poor Albert. But enough, Pilpenny! I don't want to think about any of that any more tonight. Let's have a murder instead, shall we?'

'Oh, yes. It's been days and days since we had one.'

CHAPTER 36

The Third Trunk

Nula's trunk was packed tightly and nearly over-
flowing. When I asked her if her trunk was that full
when she came to America, she looked at me as if I
were completely out of my mind.

'I can tell you exactly what was in this trunk when I sailed
for America: two ill-fitting dresses, an apron, a nightshirt, a
raggedy quilt, a few photographs, a bag of soil and a packet of
seeds.'

'That's all?'

'That's all. The soil was from our yard in Ireland. The seeds
were, I thought, flower seeds, but turned out to be carrot seeds.
The quilt I stole from my parents' bed and the dresses and
photographs I stole from my sister.'

Lizzie looked as if she'd swallowed a mouse. 'You *stole* those
things?'

There was a look on Nula's face I'd not seen before: sly, like a fox.

'I figured I deserved them. After all, my parents were stealing my family and my life from me – that's what I thought at the time – and my sister had stolen the one boy I loved with all my young heart.'

Lizzie was nearly beside herself with shock. 'She stole a *boy*? How did she steal a boy? Did she kidnap him? Why wasn't she arrested? How can somebody steal somebody like that?'

'She didn't kidnap him, Lizzie,' Nula said. 'She stole his *heart*.'

Lizzie's right hand clasped her chest protectively.

'You know I don't mean his *actual* heart, don't you, Lizzie?'

Lizzie sat up straight. 'Of *course*. I know *that*.'

'It was Finn, wasn't it?' I said.

'*Finn!*' Lizzie echoed. 'That boy *Finn*!'

'Finn,' Nula agreed. 'That boy Finn, that wicked boy Finn.'

'But why would you love a wicked boy instead of a nice boy?' Lizzie asked. 'What did he do? Did he kill someone? Steal something?'

'He stole hearts,' Nula said. 'He told lies.'

Lizzie's face was scrunched up like a dried apricot. 'So your sister stole Finn, and you stole those dresses – was everyone going around *stealing* things?'

'Lizzie, when you put it that way, I suppose so. Yes. A lot of stealing going on.' She reached into the trunk. 'We are going to have to speed this up or we'll be here for days.' As she pulled a large, tissue-wrapped parcel from the top, she sat back on her heels, gently patting the tissue and pressing the parcel to her.

'Joe,' she whispered. 'Joe, Joe, Joe.'

I closed my eyes and touched the tissue and saw him coming across the field.

'My wedding dress,' Nula whispered. She set the parcel to one side and stared at the trunk. Tentatively, she reached back inside, withdrawing an envelope, which she opened.

'Dried-up roses from the garden. Why would I save those?' She seemed to press on with renewed determination. 'What's this? Ah, these two crows – somebody sent them to me – I have no idea who. Maybe a secret admirer?' Nula handed one of the crows to me and one to Lizzie.

Lizzie said, 'Why crows? They don't seem like a very romantic thing to send.'

The one I held fit smoothly in my palm. It was heavier than I expected, maybe made of iron, and it looked vaguely familiar. Maybe Nula had kept the pair in the house at one time.

Nula pulled a faded quilt from the trunk. 'Here's the raggedy quilt I told you about. And here, these are the two dresses I stole from my sister, and the photographs, and here is that pouch of soil from Ireland, from our yard – I have to smell it, I *have* to.'

She clutched the bag to her. I thought she might break down again, but instead she smiled the broadest smile, the first true smile I'd seen on her face in a long time.

'It's just dirt, right?' Lizzie said.

Nula dipped her fingers in the bag, removing a small portion of the dirt. 'Smell,' she said, offering it to Lizzie and then to me. 'Smell that? That's *Ireland*.'

It did smell different from Blackbird Tree dirt, I admit, more mushroomy or something.

'And these?' I reached for two photographs. Both were faded and crinkled, as if they'd been carried around for some time. The one on top was larger. In it, six children – three girls and three boys – stood in various stages of awkwardness in front of a fat oak tree. All of them were barefoot; all wore shapeless clothes.

Nula peered at the photograph. 'This feels strange. That's me, that skinny one there, and that's Riley and this one's Malachy. They both died in the war. Here are Thomas and little Norah, who both died from influenza the year after this photograph was taken.'

She held the photograph closer to her face and then held it an arm's length away; back and forth she moved it, peering at it.

'But who's that?' I asked. 'That other girl next to you.'

'And where are your parents?' Lizzie asked. 'Why aren't they in the picture?'

'They didn't want to be. They were embarrassed, I think, or maybe superstitious.' Nula said a travelling photographer had come through their village and one of her sisters begged her parents to have the photograph taken. 'She wanted that photograph so badly. She wanted to see what she looked like – what she looked like to someone else. And then, when she saw the final photograph, she nearly tore it up. She cried and cried. "I look so *poor*," she wailed.'

'Which sister was that – was it the one next to you, the one with the flower in her hair?' I asked.

'Yes. That's her.'

'What's her name?'

'Sybil.'

'And what happened to her? Did she die, too?'

'I've no idea. Probably married the wretched Finn.'

I had already turned to the second photograph, but Lizzie was horrified by what Nula had said. 'What? You have *no idea* what happened to your sister? How can that be?'

'We lost touch,' Nula said, with ice in her voice.

Lizzie persisted. 'That is too entirely tragic. Is she still in Ireland?'

'I've no idea.'

'But don't you want to find out? Haven't you tried to locate her?'

'We had a falling-out, Lizzie.'

'But what if she's sick and only has a week to live? Wouldn't it be enormously tragic if she was still alive and maybe ailing and pining for her sister and time is ticking away and her sister – you – don't find her in time?'

Nula pressed her fingertips to her forehead. 'Lizzie, Lizzie, you sure have a lot of questions.'

'Naomi, what do *you* think? Don't you think Nula should — What's the matter, Naomi? What are you looking at? Is that the other picture Nula stole? Who is it? Who's in it?'

My voice came out of my mouth as if it had escaped from the body of a toad. 'Finn?'

Lizzie snatched the photo from me and stuck her face right up against it.

Nula said, 'You're right, Naomi, good guess.'

CHAPTER 37

Return to the Unfortunates

No sooner had we finished going through Nula's trunk than the chickens stirred up a racket outside. From below came a woman's voice.

'Lizzie? Naomi? Mrs Mudkin sent me.' The church secretary was standing amid the chickens, kicking at them. 'Go on. Shoo, shoo.'

'Uh-oh,' Lizzie said. 'Is today Tuesday?'

'It *is*,' the secretary said. 'It's Tuesday and you didn't show up for the unfortunates.'

On the way to Mr Canner's house, I again showed Lizzie the photograph of Nula's Finn. 'Does that look like Finn to you?'

'How would I know?'

'No, I mean does it look like *my* Finn?' I was stunned that I had said '*my* Finn,' that I'd said it aloud, but Lizzie didn't blink.

'It's all faded and fuzzy, Naomi.'

'But *look* at it. Does that boy look like *my* Finn?' This time I said it purposefully – *my* Finn.

Lizzie squinted. She puckered her lips. She opened her eyes widely.

'No.'

'But are you *sure*?'

'Oh, Naomi, I don't know! Don't ask me things like that, especially when you know how I am feeling, all lost and alone and afraid and about to be homeless.'

We had reached Mr Canner's house, and there was Mrs Mudkin standing on the top step, tapping her fingers against the porch pillar.

'Girls, I need to be able to count on you. Now take this bell.' She shoved the old school bell at me. 'Ring when you're done and don't you be in too much of a hurry. I'll be next door visiting.'

Mr Canner was grumpy that we were late. He scolded Lizzie for having thrown out his mail the last time we were there. 'Don't throw anything out today, missy. You understand?'

I was reminded of Joe. He would sometimes say 'Listen, missy,' but he was always joking when he used that word *missy*. 'Listen here, missy,' he might say, 'I'm not as old as you think,' and 'Listen up, missy – I was quite a looker in my day.'

In the last few days, when Joe tapped at the door of my brain like this, he was always *still there*. He was still alive, but *somewhere else*, maybe out in the fields or in the barn.

Mr Canner was dressed up again, this time in a white shirt with a stiff collar, a plaid handkerchief around his neck, a shiny black waistcoat, perfectly ironed grey trousers and polished black shoes. He gestured to the side table and said to me, 'Go on, read from that one on top. Start where the bookmark is.'

I opened the book and flipped to the bookmarked page. I looked at the title of the story and then around the room.

'Go on,' Mr Canner said. 'Bird got your tongue?'

The title of the story was 'The Legend of Finn McCoul'. If the house was on fire, if an earthquake shook the rafters, if a hurricane battled the windows, I was not about to leave Mr Canner's house until I had read the story of Finn McCoul.

I'd no sooner read the first few lines than Mr Canner interrupted.

'Aye, Finn McCoul, one of my favourites.' Mr Canner was less pinched today; his head even seemed less pointy. He settled back into his chair. 'Continue, continue.'

And so I continued the tale of Finn McCoul, an Irish hero, a giant of a man who lived with his equally large wife, Oonagh, in a castle at the top of Knockmany Hill. No man could beat Finn, and Finn feared no man. Only one thing did he fear: the giant Cucullin, who was said to be bigger and stronger than Finn himself.

'It's a good story, i'nnit?' Mr Canner said at various points. 'I do like a good story.'

One day Finn learned that the giant Cucullin was coming for Finn, and Finn rushed home, supposedly to check on his wife, Oonagh, but in truth, to see if she could help him.

'Listen to what she does,' Mr Canner said.

Oonagh devised a plan. When Cucullin arrived, Finn was in a cradle pretending to be their child. After several other clever tricks, Oonagh invited Cucullin to see the child. Cucullin was horrified to think that if Finn's child was this big, how enormous must the adult Finn be? The tale ended with Cucullin fleeing Knockmany Hill, vowing never to return.

'Ho, that's a grand tale, i'nnit? That Finn was a mighty man.'

'Seems to me it was his wife who was mighty.'

'What?' Mr Canner's face resumed its pinched prune shape.

'She was the one who used her brains to save her husband.'

'*Fuh.* You don't know anything about Finn McCoul.'

Lizzie joined us. '*Another* Finn?'

Next we walked to Pork Street to attend to one-armed Farley in Mrs Broadley's boarding house. We approached with caution, given that the last time we were here, Mr Farley had become agitated about seeing the King of Ireland. We found him hunched in his armchair dressed in the same clothes we'd last seen him in: blue jeans, red flannel shirt and brown slippers. He didn't seem to remember us.

'What do you want with me?'

Mrs Mudkin explained our presence. '. . . and so the girls are here to help you with anything, little or large. How's that? What would you like them to do?'

Mr Farley did not answer. He stared down at his brown slippers. I wanted to fly out of the window, be anywhere but there in that stuffy and stuffed room that smelled of furniture polish. In the china cabinet were Mrs Broadley's fragile dishes and figurines, the cabinet like a time capsule, the whole room like a time capsule, with Mr Farley as the human exhibit. And then I saw the iron birds again. I bent closer. Two crows.

I tugged at Lizzie's sleeve. 'Look in there. See anything strange?'

'What? That Eiffel Tower? That little bunny?'

'No, there, those crows.'

'What about them?'

'Aren't they like the ones Nula had in her trunk? The ones from the secret admirer?'

'Naomi, what are you talking about?'

'The crows – the ones in Nula's trunk.'

We both glanced at Mr Farley, who was still studying his slippers.

Mrs Mudkin scolded me and Lizzie for whispering. 'Girls, if you have something to say, say it so we can all hear.'

I inched towards Mr Farley. 'Mr Farley, those things in the cabinet, did you say they belonged to Mrs Broadley?'

'What cabinet?'

'That one, over there.'

'Not my stuff.'

'None of it?'

'None of it.'

'Not even those two crows?'

'No.'

'So those crows belong to Mrs Broadley?'

'No.'

'But you said — if they don't belong to you and they don't belong to Mrs Broadley, then who—'

'Raynee, please stop pestering Mr Farley. It isn't polite.'

'*Naomi*. My name is *Nay-oh-me*, and I wasn't pestering him. I was making conversation.'

'It sounds a lot like pestering, Naymee.'

'Mary,' Mr Farley said.

'What?'

'Mary-Mary.'

I felt as if I'd been flung into a busy market square in the middle of a foreign city and all around me people were spouting unintelligible words: '*Zucchopeno! Mitzolaka! Radeetska!*'

'Mary-Mary,' Mr Farley repeated. 'Mary-Mary-Mary-Mary-Mary-Mary.' And then louder, 'MARY-MARY-MARY-MARY! MARY-MARY-MARY-MARY! LISTEN TO ME!'

'Come, girls, out, out,' Mrs Mudkin ordered. 'Out, out.' She ushered us into the hall and closed the door. 'I will speak with Mrs Broadley. I'm terribly afraid that Mr Farley needs more help than we can give. We seem only to agitate the poor man.'

CHAPTER 38

The Wind Blows

Joe could tell the direction of the wind just by inhaling the air. 'Smell that cedar? That's a southern wind blowin'.' If he smelled grass, it was a western wind; the smell of the riverbank meant a northern wind; and the smell of sand and ocean told of the eastern wind.

On the way home from Mr Farley's the wind was strong, pushing bits of paper into the air like so many little white birds fluttering. 'Sand, ocean,' I said. 'Eastern wind blowing.'

'How do you know that?' Lizzie asked. 'I couldn't tell you east from west, I never could, I get so mixed up and turned round. *Lar-de-dar!* That wind!' She turned her back to it and grabbed hold of my arm. 'Naomi, I'm so scared. Why don't the Cupwrights want me? Honestly, Naomi, if I didn't have you, I'd be all alone in this world, completely and totally alone, do you know what that means? I've got to go home now but I don't really even have a home any more, do I? I have to go back there to that place and wonder when they will get rid of me. Will it be today? Or tomorrow? The next day?'

I almost told her to stop asking me questions, but instantly I thought of Joe saying that Lizzie could talk the ears off a cornfield, and it made me laugh, and I wrapped an arm around Lizzie.

'I won't let you be homeless, you crawdad.'

'I know it,' she said. 'After all, my mother probably saved your *life*. See you later! Ooh, that wind!'

The wind barrelled down the street, swirling grit along the edges of the road and up over the kerbs and into our faces. The wind whipped against shutters and slammed screen doors.

I knew I would see Finn after I left Lizzie, and I did. I knew he would be just beyond Tebop's store, and he was. I knew we would walk along the creek with the eastern wind blowing, and we did.

Against the shelter of a big oak tree, we were protected from the wind as it whirled around us and snapped through the tall grass. When I pressed Finn about where he was from, he told me Duffayn.

'Duffayn?' I said. 'Have I heard of that before?'

He leaned his forehead against mine. 'You're asking *me*?'

'I was trying to place where it was—'

'Ireland.'

Two thoughts popped into my head. One was that Finn might leave as suddenly as he had arrived. The other was that I wanted to go beyond Blackbird Tree and its cocoon of protection and its people rooted to that small patch of earth.

When I left Finn, I returned to Mr Farley's.

'Mr Farley, I'm sorry to bother you again—'

'Everybody bothers me.'

'I'm sorry about that, but may I ask you one question?'

'Everybody asks me questions.'

'Yes. Well.' I was standing beside the china cabinet.

'Were you trying to tell us that these crows belonged to Mary-Mary?'

'Mary-Mary!' His fingers fluttered towards me. 'Mary-Mary!'

'May I see the crows? May I hold them?'

With less effort than I expected, Mr Farley pulled himself from his chair, retrieved a key from a desk drawer, opened the cabinet and handed me the crows.

Mr Farley returned to the desk and rummaged through a deep bottom drawer. From it, he pulled a blue box, and from the stack of papers inside, he withdrew a white envelope and offered it to me.

It was a note addressed to Mary (not Mary-Mary).

I do not know who sent them to me. I do not know why anyone would send me crows. Crows! Knowing how much you love birds, though, I thought you might like to have them.

I glanced at the signature, too flowery to decipher, and reread the note. I was about to replace the note in the envelope when I felt a tiny jolt, as if there were an electrical charge to the letter. I looked more closely at the signature. I made out the first name: *Margaret*. The last name began with an *S*.

'Margaret?' I said to Mr Farley. 'Did you know this Margaret?'

'No.'

I studied the signature again. *S. Se*. Or *Sc*. It looked a little like *Strawberry* or *Sheltering*.

The wind was behind me as I raced for home; I felt as if it might lift me into the air and send me halfway to the moon. I had big thoughts to match the big wind. I wondered if things that might seem frightening could lose their hold over you. I wondered if we find the people we need when we need them. I wondered if we attract our future by some sort of invisible force, or if we are drawn to it by a similar force. I felt I was turning a corner and that change was afoot.

CHAPTER 39

Side Trips

I had intended to go straight home, but my feet took me on two side trips. The first was to Witch Wiggins's house, a narrow, tall, grey clapboard house with a wide front porch. If you had to guess which house a witch lived in, this would be it. The house tilted to one side, as if eavesdropping on its neighbour. Sunburned patches of paint peeled in limp layers. The upper-storey black shutters were closed, blocking daylight from entering; the lower shutters banged in the wind. There was but a small front yard, its grass brown. Guarding the base of the house were various stone elves, toads and mushrooms.

She did not answer my knocks at the door right away. From within came tiny thumps and bumps, as if bats were knocking into walls and windows. Something thudded closed from within. A coffin? At last, latches clicked and the door inched open, held in suspension by a thick brass chain.

She was dressed in purple from head to toe: purple beret, purple sweater, long purple skirt, purple slippers. Her wiry grey hair reached halfway down her back and her face bore a thousand wrinkles. She unlatched the chain and invited me in.

'I won't bite,' she said, and then added, 'probably.'

The wind blew me into the darkened parlour. Heavy crimson curtains hung at the windows, lending a bloodstained glow to the sofa and chairs. The pendulum of a tall grandfather clock beat steadily. No coffins. Into the room flew two yellow birds, followed quickly by a green one and a blue one. They circled me. I may have ducked.

'Nothing to be afraid of,' Witch Wiggins said. 'Sweet little parakeets.' She clicked her tongue and one landed on her arm, another on the top of her head. I felt one alight on my own head. The fourth strutted across the top of the sofa.

'Do you have any crows?' I asked.

'Crows? Of course. Lots.'

'Could I see them?'

'*See* them? Of course you can see them. Anyone can *see* them.' She motioned to the window. 'Open your eyes, girl.'

'I didn't mean *real* crows, or at least not outside crows. I meant pet crows, or, no, what I really meant was not live crows—'

'Dead crows? You think I have dead crows here?' She cupped one of the parakeets in her hand, stroking its feathers with her thumb.

'No, no, carved ones. Figurines.'

Witch Wiggins stroked the bird in her hand. 'Hmm, no, I

don't believe I do. Are you looking for some? Do you collect them?'

'No.' I had been sneaking glances around the room, but apparently I was more obvious than I thought.

'You think I'm really a witch, don't you?'

'No, no. Are you?'

'Aren't we all?' She laughed, a perfect witch cackle. 'It's lovely for people to think I'm a witch. I'm quite happy for that because they steer clear of me and they don't dare cross me.' The wind banged the shutters against the house. 'There – that wind – my doing, of course.' She smiled. 'Tell me about the crows.'

And so I told her about the crows in Nula's trunk, and when I finished, she said, 'Ah, *those* crows. Those crows certainly were a bad itch for Joe. He hated those crows, hated not knowing who had sent them.'

'Do *you* know who sent them?'

The shutters banged fiercely against the house.

'I've had enough of that wind. I'll stop it soon.' She wiggled her fingers at the window. 'Takes about ten minutes.' She clicked her tongue. 'Won't Nula be wondering where you are?' Witch Wiggins ushered me to the door.

'But—'

'Don't worry, you'll know soon, bye-bye.' She eased me through the doorway and closed and latched the door behind me.

The wind pushed me along, this way and that, right up to Crazy Cora's house, and as soon as I'd climbed the porch steps, the wind calmed.

I knocked at the door and waited. Soon there came a tap-tapping and I could see, behind the lace curtain on the door window, a hunched figure making its way down the hall towards me. Her face pressed against the curtain.

Crazy Cora shouted, 'WHAT YOU WANT?'

'Uh—'

'IS THAT LADY WITH YOU?'

'No, I'm all alone.' This was maybe not a good thing to admit to a crazy person.

Crazy Cora fumbled with the lock and tugged at the door. 'YOU'LL HAVE TO PUSH A LITTLE. IT GETS STUCK.'

Even as I was pushing my way in, I wondered what I would say, not at all sure why I was there.

Crazy Cora wore a shapeless and faded yellow-flowered dress partly covered by a stained blue apron. Her feet were clad in pale blue bunny slippers. She was short and hunched and our eyes were nearly level.

'What do you want, girl? What are you selling? I ain't buying any. I don't want any. I don't need any.'

'I'm not selling anything.'

'Are you checking up on me? If you are, I don't have any. I haven't had a dog since Joe stole mine.'

'I'm not-I didn't — Did Joe really steal your dog?'

'Course he did. You think I'm lying?'

'No, I just can't believe he would do that.'

Crazy Cora pulled a pair of glasses from her apron pocket, settled them on her face, and peered at me. 'Well, he did. He stole Raven in the dead of night.'

'Raven? Like the black bird? Like a crow?'

'Girl, what's the matter with you? Look, you don't need to apologize for Joe. He was out of his mind with worry and he had to do something. I was mad as a bull that's stepped on a nail, but I understood. Eventually.'

I hadn't come there to apologize for Joe, but I didn't think I should say so.

A buzzer went off somewhere down the hallway.

'Got biscuits in the oven. Goodbye. Go on, now, go—' She stood there as I crossed the porch. 'Maybe some day we can have dogs in this here place again.'

CHAPTER 40

Across The Ocean: A Prowler

Mrs Kavanagh

'Pilpenny, quick, get me the gun! We've got a prowler.' Mrs Kavanagh was in her wheelchair in the front courtyard. 'Get the holler tube, too.'

She had been alerted to the prowler by the dogs, now baying near the wee cottage, and she had seen the flap of the man's jacket as he ducked behind the water barrels.

'I know exactly who it is,' she told Pilpenny as she took the gun and the megaphone. 'That fool McCoul.'

'Again? Persistent fellow, that one.'

Mrs Kavanagh shouted through the megaphone. 'PADDY McCOUL! I'LL SET THE DOGS ON YE IF YE DON'T COME OUT AND SHOW YOUR FACE.'

Silence.

'OR MAYBE I'LL SHOOT YE FIRST.' She fired two shots into

the treetops, alarming a pair of rooks and sending them flapping across the cloudy sky.

A piece of cloth waved from behind the barrels. 'Truce! I call truce!'

'LET ME SEE YOUR DIRTY FACE.'

'Aw, Sybil – 'tis but me, Finn—'

'LET ME SEE THAT FACE, AND I'M NOT SYBIL TO YOU ANY MORE, AND YOU ARE NOT FINN TO ME ANY MORE.'

'Aw, Syb—aw—' Paddy McCoul limped out into the open, pushed by Sadie and Maddie.

'Wheel me closer, Pilpenny, if you please, but not too close.'

Paddy McCoul hung his shaggy head and scuffed his shoes in the dirt.

'You never did deserve the name of Finn, you wretch. All along you were a Paddy.'

'Aw, Syb—'

'I'll tell ye what, Paddy McCoul,' Mrs Kavanagh said. 'I am bound to be rid of ye and so ye can carry off that trunk in due time. Not now, but in due time.'

Pilpenny nudged the kindling into place. 'You are looking pale, Sybil. I'll start a fire and get us some sherry, mmm?' Pilpenny watched as the fire took hold. 'Mmm, Sybil? Some sherry? Then perhaps a murder, mmm? Do you want a *Poirot* tonight or *Miss Marple*?' She turned to Mrs Kavanagh. 'Sybil? Sybil?'

CHAPTER 41

News

One morning, shortly after Nula and I had finished breakfast, we heard the chickens squawking outside, announcing a visitor.

A man's voice called, 'Hello? Hello? Anyone about?'

From the window, I could see the man. 'It's that Dingle Dangle man,' I whispered. 'Are we home?'

'Let's hide,' Nula said.

But the man was persistent. 'Hello?' He rapped at the front door. 'Anyone home?'

'Ah, well,' Nula whispered. 'Go on, you can skittle out the back if you want.'

'You sure you don't want me to stick around?'

'I'm sure. I think I can handle a dapper man.'

I stood by the back door long enough to hear the man say, 'I'm Solicitor Dingle, ma'am,' and then I slipped across the fields and over the meadow and down to the creek to dig for clay. I was surprised that Finn did not appear, but it was good to be there by myself. Near silence: with only the sounds of the birds, the water, and skittering squirrels. The squish of clay between my fingers. I fashioned two crows from the clay and perched them on a boulder to dry in the sun.

Nula was waiting for me on the porch.

'Naomi, lass, I have some news for you. You had better come in and sit down. It is unexpected news, curious news.' She pulled me into the kitchen. 'Let's have tea.'

'Tell me, Nula.'

'Where to start? OK, first: the Dingle man was here, remember?'

'Sure.'

'No, maybe I should start with—'

'Nula, please!'

'Yes, yes, so here it is: my sister Sybil is dead.'

'I thought you knew that.'

'I was wrong before, but now she really *is* dead.'

'I'm sorry, Nula.'

'I didn't think I'd cry at such news, but...'

I got her some tissues and patted her back.

'That Dingle man told you? How did *he* know?'

'Seems he knows a lot about us, Naomi.'

I couldn't imagine what there was to know about us that

would be of any interest to anyone else.

'I suppose we have to go,' Nula said.

'Go where?'

'Ireland, didn't I say? We've been summoned.'

'Ireland? As in Ireland-Ireland? The country? Why?'

'Like I said, we've been summoned to Sybil's funeral. The Dingle man has arranged everything.'

'But the house here – the barn – the chickens—'

'That, too. The Dingle man will take care of everything – and he will not say where the money is coming from. Certainly not from Sybil, I'm sure.'

I knew of no other Ireland than the Ireland of Nula's and Mr Canner's stories. It was full of fairies and elves that could lure you down deep, dark holes. There were ogres who chopped off the heads of a dozen men in a single stroke and giants who caught thunderbolts.

'Naomi, I hate to admit this, what with Sybil being newly dead and all, but I would love to see the soil of Ireland and the trees of Duffayn again.'

'Then I guess you should go.'

'We, Naomi. We would both go.'

'Ireland? The real Ireland? I wonder what Lizzie is going to say.'

Nula gasped. '*Tch!* I forgot to tell you about Lizzie! I can't believe I forgot – it's all too much, Naomi. How could I forget to tell you *that*?'

CHAPTER 42

Lar-de-dar Lar-de-dar

Before Nula could explain about Lizzie, we heard her coming.

'Lar-de-dar, lar-de-dar, lar-de-DAR! Naomi, Naomi!'

Nula's fingers pressed against her cheeks. 'I do wish I'd had a chance to tell you first.'

'Tell me *what*? *What?*'

Lizzie burst in through the door. 'Naomi, Naomi! It's like a miracle! It's like a dream!' She grabbed my shoulders and spun me around. 'Do you *believe* it? I couldn't hardly believe my ears. At first, of course, I was scared to death – the things that ran through my head – how could they possibly do this to me? And I said, "No, no, no, never!" but then when they explained everything, I thought I must be in dreamland or hallucinating because things like this never happen to me, as you well know—'

Nula's fingers were now pressed against her lips. She glanced from me to Lizzie to the ceiling and back to me again.

'—and, Naomi, I still am not entirely certain it was not a dream. Tell me it isn't a dream. Tell me.'

'Tell you *what* isn't a dream?'

'You silly, don't tease me like that. I was feeling so terribly sorrowful, what with the Cupwrights saying they couldn't adopt me and all, and I was that close to being a completely homeless person sleeping in a cardboard box with not even a pillow or a blanket and maybe only a can of beans for dinner or maybe not even that, maybe a little cat food left in a can in the trash, and—'

Nula was tapping her foot, looking at the ceiling.

'—I know I am talking too much, but I am so excited I can hardly contain myself, and I knew you would be excited, too, and—'

'Lizzie, stop. Stop talking. Now. Tell me why you are so excited.'

Lizzie squinted at me. She turned to Nula and back to me. 'Can I talk now?'

'Yes.'

'I think you are acting a little odd, Naomi. I thought surely you would be excited, what with the news and all.'

'*Which* news, Lizzie?'

'Naomi, you goof. You goof of goofness. OK, I will play your game. I am excited for the most obvious of reasons: that we're going to Ireland! Ireland!'

A thousand thunderbolts slammed to earth. A little voice came out of my mouth.

'We? *We're* going…?'

CHAPTER 43

Across the Ocean: Ireland

The first sight of Ireland was from the aeroplane window. Below lay rolling green land, pieces stitched together with seams of rock walls and hedges. As we floated down, down from the sky, the land rose up.

A driver had been sent to meet us. He was grey-haired, short and nimble and introduced himself. 'I am Patrick and so is every fourth man in Ireland, and the ones in between are named Sean or Mick or Finn, and I'll be driving you.'

At least that is what I *think* he said because he spoke so fast and in such a way that Lizzie and I could barely understand him. We must have said 'Pardon?' nine thousand times. Nula, however, had no trouble at all and when she talked with Patrick she sounded more like him than like us.

For three hours, we careened along narrow, curved roads – on the wrong side. There were no giants or ogres or elves in sight.

Sheep grazed on hilly green land and in flat pastures; silvery lakes rose up round winding curves. Soon the hum of the car, the calm of the passing landscape and the monotonous dribbling of Lizzie's chatter lulled me to sleep.

I dreamed a vivid dream. Finn was on the far side of a meadow, waving to me, calling me to join him. I started across the field, but soon my feet were weighted with mud, and Lizzie was pushing at me.

'Don't push,' I said. 'You'll make me go in deeper.'

'Naomi, I'm trying to wake you up. We are here! Wake up, you dozy goof. You are not going to believe your eyeballs!'

We were stopped at the end of a gravel drive between two stone gateposts.

'Ah, no, Patrick, this is not the place,' Nula said.

'Ma'am?'

Nula rustled in her handbag. 'Here, it says, let me find it – here – here it is: Rooks Orchard is where we're supposed to be. *Rooks Orchard*. I expect it's a little cottagey place, Patrick.'

Patrick shook his head. 'Beg'r pardon, Ma'am, this is the place you're to be delivered.' He indicated a wrought iron sign above the stone pillars. 'See there?'

We all craned to see. The sign, in bold back letters, read:

ROOKS ORCHARD

On top of each of the pillars was a tall, black bird.

I nudged Lizzie. 'Crows. See there?'

'Rooks, we call 'em,' said Patrick.

I felt as if a marble were bouncing around in my head. *Rooks Orchard?*

Nula was wiping her forehead with a handkerchief. She studied the sign and peered down the drive. 'Ah,' she said at last. 'There – see that little cottage to one side – over there – see? I bet that's where we're going. Drive on over to that cottage, Patrick, please.'

Patrick took off his cap, smoothed his hair and replaced the cap. What he replied sounded at first like '*Mamegginardonbeetinsurrec –* ' but I think that what he said was actually this: 'Ma'am, beggin' your pardon, but my instructions clearly say to take you and the lasses to the main house, and so if you'll bear with me a few minutes longer, I'll run you up there and enquire on your behalf.'

CHAPTER 44

Pilpenny

We stared up at the stone building, three storeys high and as wide as five barns. A broad gravel drive curved up to the front entrance with its tall double doors. Perfectly sculpted bushes lined the drive, and hundreds of rosebushes bloomed pink and white along a path leading from the main house to the small cottage.

Near the car bloomed a vast expanse of purple flowers. 'Lavender,' Nula whispered. 'How I have missed lavender.' She turned to Patrick. 'I suppose you have to obey your instructions, so you may pull on up to that main entrance, but I expect you will be told in no uncertain terms to take us around the back. Girls, stay put, don't go jumping out of the car like a couple of jack rabbits.'

As the car crunched up the drive, Nula said, 'There is something vaguely familiar about this place. I don't know what it is, but I feel as if I've seen it before, maybe in a dream or a photograph.'

Patrick stopped the car in front of the main entrance, climbed the dozen stone steps to the porch and pulled a long bell cord beside the door.

Nula said, 'Girls, this is so embarrassing. I can't even watch. What will their butler think, with us presuming to come to the door like this, unannounced.'

One of the doors opened, revealing a trim, dark-haired woman who greeted Patrick. She nodded and then looked to the car where we sat, huddled like three stowaways. The woman clasped her hands together and walked towards us, neither smiling nor frowning.

'So embarrassing,' Nula said.

The woman tapped at the window. Nula rolled it down and said, 'I'm so sorry we've troubled you—'

The woman was peering round Nula, eyeing me and Lizzie. One of her slender fingers reached in and pointed at Lizzie. 'You are Lizzie, am I correct?'

Lizzie shrank back against me.

The finger pointed to me. 'And you must be Naomi, correct? And you' – now she tapped Nula's shoulder – 'you must be Nula, correct?'

We three nodded dumbly.

The woman beamed. 'Marvellous!' she said. 'And me, I am Miss Pilpenny.'

'You?' Lizzie croaked.

What I had learned on the day that Nula told me we'd been summoned to Ireland was that Lizzie had also been summoned, but by someone else. That someone else was her mother's sister, a Miss Pilpenny, the woman that Lizzie used to refer to as her mother's 'crazy' sister.

At first Lizzie had refused this surprise invitation. 'Absolutely not,' she told Mr Dingle. 'I am not going across the ocean to see a crazy person.'

Mr Dingle assured Lizzie that Miss Pilpenny was not crazy at all, and that by an odd stroke of fate (which he'd helped along), Miss Pilpenny had been a companion to Nula's sister, Sybil Kavanagh. Mr Dingle also informed Lizzie that Nula and I would be travelling with her.

'Is that *true*, really and truly *true*?' Lizzie said she'd replied to Mr Dingle. 'If that's really and truly true, then of course I will go.'

Nula tried to prepare us for the worst. 'Accommodations in Ireland are not generally as grand as they are in America,' she said. 'Things are smaller and older, very much older. The ceilings are low. The rooms are dark and damp.'

By the time we got on the plane, I was expecting that we'd be staying in a root cellar, with hay for bedding.

Now, on Irish soil, Miss Pilpenny stood outside the car and crossed her hands on her chest, exactly as Lizzie did sometimes. 'Oh, my stars! I can hardly believe you're here.'

'You do *look* like my mother,' Lizzie said. 'You even sound a little like her. *You* are Auntie Pilpenny?' I knew what Lizzie was thinking: *You don't* look *crazy!*

'Come, come,' Miss Pilpenny said, tugging at the door handle. 'You must be tired from your travels.'

Nula said, 'But where should we go—?'

'Here,' Miss Pilpenny said. '*Here*, of course. Come along. Patrick will bring your cases.'

As we tentatively unfolded ourselves from the car, Lizzie and Miss Pilpenny studied each other.

'I hope I do not appear too entirely strange to you, Lizzie.'

For once, Lizzie was without words.

We followed Pilpenny (*Auntie* Pilpenny) into a vast hall tiled in white-and-black marble. A wide, winding staircase loomed to our right, a crystal chandelier the size of a hay bale hung from the ceiling, a wide corridor continued on the far side of the hall and a high arch to our left opened into a vast parlour with floor-to-ceiling windows framed in acres of gold silk.

'What first?' Pilpenny asked. 'Do you want a spot of tea or to freshen up or to see your rooms or to roam the grounds for some fresh air?'

Lizzie was still without words. I'd never seen her so quiet and thought maybe she was sick.

I managed to squeak out, 'Room, ma'am.' If we were going to be staying out in the barn, I wanted to know it sooner rather than later.

We followed her up the winding staircase with a hundred or more steps and along a landing lined with flowered wallpaper. Every five metres or so were closed doors on either side of the landing.

Lizzie whispered to me, 'It must be a hotel.'

Never having been in a hotel, I couldn't comment.

Nula, Lizzie and I had three adjoining rooms. Windows overlooked the back gardens and acres of green stretching towards a grove of fruit trees. My room had a fireplace; a tall cupboard that Pilpenny called a *wardrobe*; a cozy stuffed chair; and various tables and lamps. Cheery peach blossom wallpaper made the room feel like a sunny orchard.

It was too much to absorb. I climbed up on the high bed and lay down. 'I'll just be here a few minutes,' I said as I deflated like a punctured balloon into the soft pillow and soft mattress. I woke once, later, in the darkened room, not knowing where I was, and only vaguely taking in the night table with its fresh flowers before sinking back into sleep again.

I did not wake again until the next morning, when I felt something pecking at my shoulder. I opened my eyes, face-to-face with a black bird.

'It's not real,' Lizzie said. 'I've tried just about everything to wake you up, Naomi. How are you feeling? I've been up for hours. Auntie Pilpenny will try to give you some awful oatmeal mush, but ask for toast and jam and you will have the most delicious plum jam ever in this world and it is straight from the plum trees in the orchard—'

'Lizzie, stop.' I was so groggy, I couldn't fathom where I was.

Was I home in my bed? Had I been sick?

'Are you all mixed up, too, Naomi? I didn't half know where I was when I opened my eyes this morning. I thought someone had kidnapped me or that I was in a dream, and then I finally realized I was in Ireland—'

I looked closer at what Lizzie was holding. 'Is that a crow?'

'It's a rook. Remember what Patrick said yesterday? That's the name of this place, remember that? *Rooks Orchard*.'

CHAPTER 45

The Bridge and the Orchard

Like me, Nula had slept late that morning. 'I'm a little disoriented,' she said at breakfast.

'More plum jam?' Pilpenny asked.

Lizzie said, 'See if I have this straight. Nula and Mrs Kavanagh – Sybil – were sisters, and Auntie Pilpenny and my mother were sisters.'

That part was fairly simple.

'So Pilpenny is my aunt, but Naomi's not really related to anybody.'

'Am, too,' I said. 'I'm related to Joe and Nula.'

Nula sat forward, then back, then forward again, as if she were about to speak.

Lizzie jumped in first. 'No, you're not,' Lizzie persisted. 'You're not related by *blood*.'

'What difference does *that* make?'

'I'm just saying – just getting things clear in my own head – that I am definitely related to someone who is alive—'

'Sometimes,' I said, 'you might want to keep your thoughts in your own head.'

Nula and Pilpenny exchanged helpless looks, as if they could sense that war might break out at any moment.

'How about some air?' Pilpenny said. 'Let's have a walkie, shall we?'

Pilpenny, with Lizzie at her side, led the way along the wide stone path. This pair, who had so recently met, seemed so natural with each other, matching each other's steps and gestures. I found myself altering my steps to be in rhythm with Nula and consciously mirroring the way her hands moved when she spoke.

'Naomi, what on earth are you doing? Are you making fun of me?'

'No, no. Sorry.'

'Are you bothered that Lizzie has found a ... relative?'

'I'm not bothered. I'm *glad* she found a relative. It makes me jumpy, though. What if someone up and claims *me*?'

Nula stopped in the middle of the path. 'You wouldn't like that?'

'No. Why would I like that? You and me and Joe, we get along fine.'

'But Joe isn't—'

'Joe's just fine.'

Nula looked up into the sky and down the path and then she turned and looked back towards the house. 'Naomi, lass, I have always worried that someone *might* come along and claim you.'

'You *worried* about it? So you would have been bothered by that?'

'Of course! That was hard on me and Joe, that worry. You were a great, unexpected surprise dropped into our lives, and it took us a long time to accept that good fortune. Maybe we kept a little too much distance sometimes, but—'

'Poor, poor, pitiful me.'

Nula picked up the routine. 'Yes, you ragamuffin lass, now pick up your feet and get a move on. We can't stand here gabbing all day.' From her pocket Nula withdrew a small packet wrapped in green cloth. Inside was another packet wrapped in plastic. 'Look who I brought along,' she said, extending her hand towards me.

At first I thought she held sand.

'It's Joe,' she said, with a crooked grin. 'I could hardly see Ireland without him, could I?'

'I thought you buried his ashes.'

'Only a few of them – the rest of his ashes are in that red cookie tin at home.' She winked at me. 'Joe and I weren't *blood related*, but we were a good match, don't you think?'

Nula took a pinch of ashes and scattered them near a clump of lavender. 'Purty, don't you think, Joe? Mmm?' From the packet she retrieved another pinch. 'Don't know anybody who knew Joe like you and I did, Naomi. We were a good match, you and me and Joe.' Nula flicked bits of Joe over a rosebush.

To one side of us stretched a vast, rolling green lawn; the other side was bordered by rosebushes, lavender and magnolia trees. At this time of morning the path was shaded by trees arching over us, and it looked as if we were entering a strange and enchanted land.

We met the gardener, a sturdy-looking man wearing work trousers, boots and a collared shirt and tie, who introduced himself as Michael. He wiped his hand on his trousers and shook each of our hands. When he came to me, he said, 'Dust yer arm hurt yer, lass?'

'No.'

'A dog ate it,' Lizzie said.

Michael-the-gardener nodded, as if that was the sort of thing he heard regularly.

Pilpenny suggested that Lizzie and I run ahead. 'If you stay on the path, you'll come to a bridge over a stream, and on the far side of the bridge is the orchard. You can run free in the orchard, except for the fairy ring, stay clear of that.'

'A real fairy ring?' Lizzie asked.

'As real as ever a fairy ring was,' Pilpenny answered. 'You won't have any trouble spotting it – it's in the middle of the orchard, beyond the sundial. Don't enter the ring.'

Lizzie said, 'Naomi, did you hear her? She said we mustn't enter the fairy ring.'

'I heard her, Lizzie. I'm not deaf.'

It felt good to run, after that long plane ride and long sleep. The air smelled of – was that salt and sand? Were we that near the ocean? It also smelled of green, green grass and of sweet fruit. We raced along the winding path, shedding our recent squabble, catching glimpses between the bushes of gentle hills and meadows, of low rock walls and stubby trees and hulking boulders. Soon we came to the stream and the most unusual wooden bridge. It did not go straight across the wide stream. Instead it jogged this way and that: left, then right, then right again, then left, right, left. You could not easily run across it because of the frequent turns.

'Did you ever see such a crooked bridge?' Lizzie asked.

'I never did in my whole life. It doesn't make any sense, does it? Do you think it makes any sense at all, Naomi?'

'Didn't Finn talk about a crooked bridge?'

'Did he?'

'He drew it in the dirt—'

'Oh, I remember. Isn't that funny? What a coincidence.'

On the far side of the crooked bridge were two tall pillars, much like those at the front entrance to the main house. On top of each pillar was a tall crow (or, as Patrick, the driver, had said, a rook) and joining the two pillars in a graceful arch was a sign in iron letters:

ROOKS ORCHARD

Beyond the entrance were row upon row of fruit trees.

'So there really is an orchard at Rooks Orchard,' Lizzie said.

'I didn't think the name of the place might actually mean something, did you, Naomi? Did you expect a real orchard? And maybe there are – look! There. Rooks!'

'*Cor, cor, cor*,' came the call of a rook overhead. '*Cor, cor, cor, cor.*' More rooks, maybe a dozen, circled above the trees.

'How about that?' Lizzie said. 'There's this enormous hotel place and plum jam and a new auntie and magnolias and roses and lavender and a crooked bridge and an orchard and rooks – there is too much coming into my head, Naomi.'

Again, the mention of the crooked bridge and now the rooks and the orchard reminded me of Finn. It was like a flash of a photograph before it disappeared.

We were surrounded by fruit trees that stretched as far as we could see. Following the path, we came to a sundial, and beyond it, the fairy ring. Mushrooms the size of my fist formed a narrow rim. The interior of the ring was a mix of grass and flowers and flattened areas that snaked through the grass.

'A real fairy's ring?' Lizzie said. 'My mother talked of fairy rings, I just remembered that. Isn't that peculiar? They dance and play music in there. No humans or animals can go inside the ring. Terrible, terrible fates befall you if you trespass on a fairy ring.'

'Like what?'

'I don't know, maybe your head would be chopped off. Maybe you would be struck blind, or maybe you would vanish altogether – *poof*!'

I balanced one foot on top of a mushroom.

'Don't, Naomi, don't do that.'

I rolled the mushroom the slightest bit under my foot.

'Don't, Naomi, please don't.'

I dipped my foot inside the ring and quickly drew it back again.

'Naomi!' Lizzie said.

'*Nay-oh-me. Lizz-ee.*' From far away someone called our names.

'Now you've done it,' Lizzie said. 'If something gets us, it's all your fault.'

CHAPTER 46

Across the Ocean: A Storm

ack in Blackbird Tree, a steady, strong wind pushed heavy grey clouds over the town. Blacker clouds and wilder winds galloped behind them, blasting leaves and limbs off trees, signs off posts, shingles off roofs. The wind howled through the town, slamming against doors and shutters. Thunder bellowed and lightning cracked overhead.

Cats slid onto porches, trash barrels banged against garages, people dived into doorways, all seemingly calling, *Let me in, let me in.*

Inside his home, Mr Canner held *Tales of Ireland* against his chest as he dozed in his chair. In Mrs Broadley's boarding house, one-armed Farley held an iron crow and whispered, 'Mary-Mary.'

Crazy Cora, face pressed against her cold bedroom window, watched a lone chicken flutter and tumble down the street.

Witch Wiggins opened all the windows in her house and let the wind race through. The curtains twirled wildly, magazines leaped into the air and flew through the rooms, and her colourful birds dived under the sofa.

A buzz was heard through the town as wires plunged to the ground and flapped like whips. The lights went out.

'It comes, it goes,' Witch Wiggins said.

CHAPTER 47

Real or Not Real?

As we returned to the main house, Lizzie said, 'Is this the only hotel in the area? Is that why we're staying in this grand place? It must cost a fortune.'

Pilpenny blinked. 'Hotel? This isn't a hotel. Did you all think—?' She gaped at us.

'What is it, then?' Lizzie said.

'It's Rooks Orchard. It's Sybil's place.'

Nula staggered backwards. 'Wha—?'

And that is how we learned that Rooks Orchard belonged to Sybil Kavanagh.

Inside, we met Dora, the cook, who offered us 'wee cakes'. To me, she said, 'Dust yer wonky arm urt yer, lass?'

'No.'

'A dog ate it,' Lizzie offered.

A bell rang at the front and Pilpenny went to answer it.

We heard a man's voice in the hall.

'Eezer slister,' the cook said.

'What?'

We looked out into the hall and saw Mr Dingle standing there.

'Eezer slister. SYBIL'S SLISTER. Yer got taters in yer ers?'

Lizzie took offence. 'We do *not* have taters in our ears. We just cannot understand you sometimes. What does "eezer slister" mean?'

'Ut means EEZER SLISTER.'

Upstairs, Lizzie was as wound up as a tin soldier. 'Naomi, what are you *thinking*? That Dingle Dangle man – that *eezer slister* – seems to know *everybody*. And I don't think Auntie Pilpenny is crazy at all, do you? I hope not, because if she is crazy, then maybe I could be crazy, too, since we are *blood relatives*—'

If the wall were closer to me, I'd have banged my head on it.

'And when you stepped in the fairy ring – oh, Naomi – well, isn't it strange that the Dingle man showed up right after that? And I'm thinking there is some bad news.'

Out of the donkey's ears . . .

'Naomi, I'm all mixed up. Are we really here? Is this real or not real?'

'What is "real"?'

'Naomi, sometimes you make me dizzy.'

I wanted to tell her that, as we were leaving the orchard earlier, I thought I had seen a boy in the shadows. For an instant, I thought I saw Finn. But I did not tell her.

I wanted to tell her what I thought I had seen at the side of the path: a flat stone, with crude markings:

But I didn't tell Lizzie because maybe the boy and the stone were not real.

CHAPTER 48

Across the Ocean: Wind and Fire

For three days the rains pelted and the winds howled through Blackbird Tree. Trees lay like fallen soldiers, signs skittered across fields, tarpaulins battered their dark wings through the air, tractors lay upended, their under-bellies exposed. Thunder raged. Lightning spiked roofs and trees.

Mr Canner slept in his chair, *Tales of Ireland* now on the floor at his feet.

One-armed Farley, in Mrs Broadley's boarding house, hid under the blue quilts on his bed, cradling the pair of iron crows.

A tree had fallen on the roof of Crazy Cora's house, crushing her bed, but not her. She was in the bathroom at the time.

As the air crackled with lightning, Witch Wiggins felt a jolt. Her whole body trembled, her hair stood on end, the air boomed with thunder. Across town she watched a giant bolt of lightning dart from the sky, crashing into a barn roof. A second bolt, even stronger, lit up the house near the barn. A few minutes later, smoke. And then, fire: the barn, the house.

The following morning, twenty or thirty residents of Blackbird Tree gathered in the yard of what had been Joe and Nula's house. What remained were charred and smoking stubs of timber; lumps of black, smouldering furniture; and a few stray, colourful items poking from the ashes – a red cookie tin, a yellow platter, a blue mug.

The chicken coop was no more; the chickens were no more. The barn was now a hill of smoking ashes, with a few ragged beams jutting up at odd angles, their pointed ends stabbing at the sky. The rounded top of a chest lay collapsed on its burned contents, like a giant turtle shell. Beneath it poked the heads of two iron crows.

Crazy Cora stood with Mrs Broadley from the boarding house and Mrs Mudkin from the church.

'One day it's all there, and the next day it's gone,' said Mrs Broadley.

'Poof!' said Crazy Cora.

'I heard they went to Ireland,' Mrs Broadley said.

'For good?'

'I've no idea.'

'Who's going to tell them?'

'No idea.'

'It was Witch Wiggins, you know.'

'Says who?'

'Ever'body.'

Mrs Mudkin closed her eyes. 'We should pray.'

'I ain't praying,' Crazy Cora said.

Mrs Mudkin said, 'Lord, please bless—'

'I ain't praying.'

'—this land and the people who—'

'I ain't praying.'

'—have toiled on this earth—'

'Stop that praying.'

'I can pray if I want to.'

'Then be quiet about it.'

CHAPTER 49

From Donkeys' Ears

We received the news of the fire that burned our house and barn.

'To the ground,' Nula told us. 'It's all, all gone.'

'The chickens?'

'The chickens, too.'

'The house, the barn? All of it?'

'Gone.'

Lizzie blurted, 'You're homeless. Oh, it's awful, awful. It's so entirely pitiful.'

And at that moment, when it felt as if bad stuff was pouring out of the donkey's ears, it did seem entirely pitiful.

CHAPTER 50

Across the Ocean: The Witch Visits

After Mrs Broadley, blue bag in hand, set off for her weekly grocery errands, Witch Wiggins entered the boarding house, always unlocked. At one-armed Farley's door, she knocked.

'Artie? You there?' she called.

'Eh? Who's that?'

'Hazel.'

The door opened quickly, as if he'd been expecting her.

'I've brought you something,' she said. On the table, she placed her parcel and unfolded the newspaper wrappings.

One-armed Farley gasped. He leaned over to study the items and then rushed to the cabinet and retrieved the two birds that had been Mary-Mary's. 'Identical!' he said, setting his two beside the pair that Hazel Wiggins had brought.

She explained that she had retrieved them from the ashes of Joe and Nula's barn. 'These are rooks, you know, not crows.'

One-armed Farley gently stroked the new rooks. He lined all four up in a row and then he rearranged them so that the old two were facing the new two. 'They will need time to get acquainted,' he said.

'Or reunited.'

One-armed Farley stared at her. 'Reunited? You mean—?'

'I think they were all together once.'

'Together.' He nodded, and then he crossed the room to a small desk, and from its centre drawer, he pulled out a piece of blue paper. He folded it carefully and handed it to Hazel Wiggins.

CHAPTER 51

Ashes

We were a small procession: Nula, carrying a black urn containing her sister's ashes; Pilpenny; the cook and the gardener; the Dingle Dangle man; and me and Lizzie. The sun shone on the wide lawn, the trees casting long shadows across the path. And so we walked between sun and shadows, until we came to the Crooked Bridge.

'Pardon me, Nula,' Pilpenny said. 'Sybil always liked me to run her across the bridge. May I?'

Nula handed the urn to Pilpenny, and off she went, urn cradled in her arms. Left, right, right. 'Whoopsie!' she called. At the far end, she said, 'There, Sybil. Once again we escaped the evil spirits.'

As we entered the iron gate with rooks atop each pillar, Pilpenny pointed out Sybil's sleek black rook circling overhead. Down the centre path we went, past apple and plum and pear trees. 'Have to pull plums before long,' Pilpenny said. 'We're a bit late on the pears.'

We passed the sundial, made a wide berth past the fairy ring and stopped at the end of the path. Pilpenny indicated a newly mown patch of meadow beyond. 'There. That's what she wanted.'

We could make out a small hole, about a third of a metre square, and two flat stones, side by side. On one stone was Sybil's name. The other stone was blank.

'Why two stones?' Lizzie asked.

Pilpenny turned to the Dingle Dangle man. 'That's best left to Mr Dingle to explain. After lunch. It's part of Sybil's revenge.'

'*Revenge?*'

'You'll see,' Pilpenny said.

After Nula placed the urn with Sybil's ashes into the hole, Pilpenny added a book. 'Sybil liked a good murder mystery,' she said. 'I think she'll enjoy this one.' The title was *After the Funeral*.

Mr Dingle shovelled dirt back into the hole and said a prayer.

'Before we go back,' Pilpenny said, 'I want to show you something.' She led us to a tall oak near the edge of the line of plum trees. At the base of the oak was a well-tended patch of grass and a smooth grey stone with crude markings:

F. M.

A squeak came from Nula. 'Is it him? Is this Finn's grave?'

'No,' Pilpenny said. 'Not long after Sybil came here to Rooks Orchard, when Finn took her wages and her heart and went along to another lass, Sybil scratched her broken heart into this stone – she was dramatic, you know.'

'Yes, I know,' Nula agreed.

'The stone used to be up there in the meadow where she is now buried, but it was moved here to mark the spot where Finn's son, Finnbarr, died.' She looked up into the branches of the oak tree. 'He fell from this very tree. Almost a man, still a boy in his heart, and a boy will climb a tree simply because it's there, won't he?'

I had an odd sensation: I saw myself back in Blackbird Tree when I was younger, falling, falling from a tree. *Maybe I died then. Maybe it only seems like I'm still alive.*

'Sad,' Nula said. 'Do you know the whereabouts of Finn, the father?'

'His grave is next to his son's in the Duffayn churchyard.'

'Alas,' Nula said.

'But he's still prowling around here. You'll see in time.'

I thought Nula might keel over. 'I will?'

'But he's still a wretch, you'll see.'

CHAPTER 52

The Great Unexpected

For the reading of Sybil Kavanagh's will, Mr Dingle assembled us in the parlour. I thought it nice of him to let me and Lizzie join Nula, Pilpenny, the cook and the gardener, and I hoped there would be surprises in the will. Maybe Mrs Kavanagh would leave everything to the cook or the gardener, or maybe even to her rook.

First Mr Dingle read through a few boring bits about Mrs Kavanagh being in her right mind when she made the will. I wondered what a *wrong* mind would be. Was I in my *right* mind or my *wrong* mind?

Then he said, 'It's very simple, really. Shall I proceed?' He didn't wait for an answer.

To Dora Capolini, my loyal cook, I leave the silver tea service, the silver candelabra and—

'—the contents of this bank account in your name,' Mr Dingle said, handing Dora an envelope, which she quickly opened.

'Oh!' Dora exclaimed, fanning herself. 'Heavens above! Now I can visit me sister! She's in Amurica, yer know.'

Mr Dingle continued:

> *To Michael Canner, my loyal gardener, I leave the*
> *gold hall clock, the gold pocket watch that belonged*
> *to my beloved Albert, and—*

'—the contents of this bank account in your name,' Mr Dingle said, handing Michael an envelope.

Shyly, Michael opened it. 'Erm. Is ert real?' he said. When Mr Dingle assured him it was, Michael-the-gardener jumped up and embraced Mr Dingle and then the cook and then Pilpenny and Nula and me and Lizzie. 'Is real! Yes?' He sat down. He leaped up again. 'I bring me brother over! He's in Amurica, isn't he, now? Yes!'

Mr Dingle then asked Dora and Michael to leave the room.

'To Nula and to Pilpenny, in equal measure,' he said, 'Sybil bequeaths bank accounts with – ahem – tidy sums.'

He passed a piece of paper to each of them.

Pilpenny merely glanced at her paper; she seemed to have already known what it contained.

A flush rose to Nula's face. 'Am I dreaming? Am I awake?' She covered her face with her hands. Pilpenny patted Nula's back.

'There's more,' Mr Dingle said. 'Sybil is very specific here. This is how she phrases it.' He then read from the will:

> *To Pilpenny, my trusted companion, and to Nula, my sister from whom I have been estranged, I bequeath the right to live in this house at Rooks Orchard and to enjoy the beauty and bounty of its lands, for so long as they shall live. I ask for one condition only: that Nula agree to be buried beside me in Rooks Orchard, and that Pilpenny look after Rook.*

'I'm not sure I completely understand,' Nula said.

'It will become clearer shortly,' Mr Dingle said. 'First, Sybil wanted you to have this.' He passed a small white box to Nula.

We all leaned forward, straining to see. Inside was an elegant gold bracelet with a single charm attached.

'Is it – is it – ah, I know!' Nula said. 'It's a rook, isn't it? So, that's who sent me those crows – those black birds – those rooks.'

'She kept track of you,' Mr Dingle said.

'Well, I never! Did I so completely misjudge my sister?'

Mr Dingle said, 'May I continue?' and again he did not wait for an answer but read directly from the will:

> *I regret the long years of estrangement from my sister Nula, all because of a wretched boy and our own foolishness.*

Nula stared at the will from which Mr Dingle was reading. 'Me, too,' she said. 'I regret it, too, Sybil.'

'There is more,' Mr Dingle said.

> *Over the years, I have developed special sympathies for young girls like we were: so full of promise but with so few opportunities.*

Mr Dingle paused here, sipping from a glass of water on the side table before he continued.

> *It is my intention to offer a better start to two young women who might most benefit: to Naomi Deane and to Lizzie Scatterding I leave this house and the entire estate of Rooks Orchard to enjoy for as long as they both shall live, with the proviso that Nula and Pilpenny be given residence, as stated above, and be treated with kindness and compassion.*

Lizzie and I stared at each other. *Real or not real?*

'There are a few more provisions,' Mr Dingle said. 'For each of you girls, there are also bank accounts, each with matching tidy sums, to be used responsibly. These accounts will be overseen by the executor of the estate, Mr C. Dingle, ahem, that is, me.' He read:

> *… the intention being that Naomi and Lizzie have the opportunity of education and travel and the ability to assist others in need of opportunity.*

'There is one proviso,' Mr Dingle added, before continuing:

> *My last request of Naomi and Lizzie is that they care*
> *for my two dogs, who have been my trusted and loyal*
> *companions. I ask that the dogs be given the best of*
> *care and the loyalty and love that they deserve and*
> *that they give so freely.*

Mr Dingle concluded: 'Sybil also leaves a sum for me as executor of the estate and a healthy bank account to provide for the maintenance of the property, the salaries of the cook and gardener, *et cetera*.'

He smiled at each of us. 'This, then, constitutes Sybil's revenge.'

'Revenge?' Nula said. 'How so?'

It was Pilpenny who answered. 'Sybil felt that, first of all, you and she were betrayed by Finn, that he took advantage of your soft hearts and your poor living conditions, stole your trust and your wages and drove a wedge between you.'

'Aye,' Nula said. 'That he did.'

'And secondly,' Pilpenny continued, 'she never forgave the wretched elderly Master Kavanagh for his treatment of her and of his son, Albert. Master Kavanagh made it clear that women had no rights of any sort and were not worth the dirt on his boots. It is, therefore, Sybil's revenge on the wretched Master Kavanagh and on the wretched Finn that women and girls will be running the estate and inheriting it.'

'Revenge?' Nula said. 'What a curious sort of revenge.'

'You mean this is *real*?' Lizzie said. 'I'm not crazy out of my mind?'

'Naomi?' Mr Dingle leaned towards me. 'You look, how shall I say? Perplexed?'

One word leaked out of my mouth: '*Dogs?*'

CHAPTER 53

One More Trunk

Maybe sudden change of any kind – even unexpected *good* fortune – jolts your world. The whole planet had tilted in an instant, and I was wobbling along at a slant, trying to regain my balance.

Nula moved about in a daze. When I asked her how she felt about Sybil's will, she said, 'I misjudged my sister, I did. I'm sorry about that, and I'm sorry I didn't see her before she died. What she has done for us, Naomi, and for Lizzie, too—'

'But what if you wanted to go back to Blackbird Tree?'

'Why would I want to do that?' she said. 'I've got you and Joe with me' – she patted her pocket – 'and a bag of Blackbird Tree dirt up in my suitcase.' She stood on the terrace overlooking the wide lawn and lavender borders. 'I've come home, haven't I?'

Lizzie was back to her talkative self. 'Naomi, I don't understand why this happened to us. *Us!* We are just two nobody girls.'

'I wouldn't exactly say "nobody", Lizzie.'

'You know what it's like? It's like out of the sky comes this thing, this great, unexpected *thing*, and it doesn't know where to land, so it lands on us, two nobody girls—'

'I wish you'd quit saying "nobody"—'

'We won't be without a home and we won't be without food and we can have new shoes on our feet and we can have a coat that fits and we can have dogs, oh, Naomi, I hope you will be OK with the dogs because if you aren't, we have to give all this up, and I have always wanted a dog, and they are so sweet, have you ever looked at their faces? Have you?'

I was worried about the dogs. I didn't know if I could do what was being asked of me. It seemed, on the surface, such a simple request, and yet when I'd close my eyes, I'd see them lunging at me. *Not real. Not real.* But the fear was real and I did not want to admit it to anyone.

Lizzie carried on: 'And there is all this green lawn and green trees and a river and a bridge and an orchard with all those good plums and pears and things, and we can go to college and be educated people, and we can help the unfortunates and—'

One afternoon I discovered that I could climb up on the roof from the balcony at the end of the upstairs landing. Up there, unexpectedly, in the wide-open air, I cried and cried, and I didn't stop to wonder why. And when the crying stopped, it felt as if someone had pulled me and Lizzie and Nula up a tall, tall ladder, and stretching out before us was all the world to see and know. I thought about the kindness of strangers. I thought about the dogs and about the great unexpected.

Below were green lawns and winding paths, roses and lavender. It seemed that everything and anything was possible. I saw a million ladders dropping down from the sky.

When I came down from the roof, Nula was standing on the balcony. 'Naomi,' she said. 'It's *OK* to accept good fortune.'

Later that day, Pilpenny asked if Lizzie and I would help her with 'a little project'. There was a trunk, she said, out in the wee cottage that needed 'some investigating'.

'Surely, we can help,' Lizzie said. 'We are good at trunks.'

Lizzie and Pilpenny seemed both amused and intrigued by each other. Lizzie told me, 'Auntie Pilpenny isn't crazy at all. She reminds me so much of my mother that it's a little spooky.' In turn, Pilpenny, watching Lizzie run and skip and twirl across the lawn, said, 'So much like my sister – her mother. So much.'

Out at the wee cottage, Pilpenny said, 'Technically, the contents of this cottage now belong to you girls, but Sybil suggested that I look through this trunk first. You girls know about Paddy – who was also called Finn – yes?'

'We know a little,' I said.

'The trunk belonged to his son, Finnbarr.'

'The dead boy?' Lizzie said. 'The one that fell out of the tree?'

'That's the one.'

Pilpenny said that many years ago Finnbarr worked in the orchards and stayed in the wee cottage, and when he died, his things were stored in that trunk.

When Pilpenny unlocked the door to the wee cottage and pushed it open, spiders dropped down from the top of the frame.

'Eww,' Lizzie said. 'I'm not so fond of spidery places.'

I stepped back when I saw tall shelves filled with rooks staring at us.

'Eww!' Lizzie said. 'That is so overly creepy!'

Pilpenny said that the Kavanaghs used to give them to guests as mementos. 'After the Master died, Sybil sent a pair to Nula—'

'Why didn't she include a note so that Nula would know who they were from?'

'That's Sybil for you. She liked mystery. I have to confess that I, too, sent a pair – without a note, a little mystery – to my sister, Margaret. That was when she was working at the hospital in Ravensworth.'

'Ohhh. So you sent them to Lizzie's mother and she gave them to Mary-Mary.'

Lizzie was confused. 'How do you know that?'

And so I told them about the note I'd seen at Mr Farley's, the one addressed to Mary and signed by Margaret S:

> *I do not know who sent them to me... Crows!*
> *Knowing how much you love birds... I thought you*
> *might like to have them.*

'Are all those rooks ours now, Auntie Pilpenny?' Lizzie asked. 'I don't mean to be piggy, but do we own all this stuff now?'

'Yes,' she said. 'But before you make big changes, you will need to consult with Mr Dingle.'

'Sure,' Lizzie said. 'We'll do that, won't we, Naomi?'

I still hadn't decided if this was real, so I was ready to agree to anything. 'Sure. Sure, we will.'

'There is a story,' Pilpenny said, 'about Finnbarr that – oh, no, I shouldn't tell—'

'Tell! I want to know *everything*!' Lizzie said.

I realized that was one difference between me and Lizzie. I didn't want to know everything that was already known; I wanted to leave room for possibilities.

Pilpenny was making her way across the room, pushing chairs and boxes out of the way. 'All right, I will tell you. It's only a tale, you know. Finnbarr – we called him Finn, like most everyone else did – had been working in the orchard for several summers. My sister, Margaret – your mother, Lizzie – and I thought he had been dropped down from heaven for us to adore and – later – quarrel over.'

Pilpenny pressed her hand against her chest, and when she made that simple gesture, it reminded me of Lizzie, and it also made me wonder if Pilpenny, too, had had her own heart wounded by a boy named Finn. Was that the fate of all girls, to have their hearts broken? Surely boys had their hearts trampled on, too, didn't they? I saw a parade in my mind: of Nula and Joe, of Sybil, of Mr Canner and one-armed Farley, of Crazy Cora and Witch Wiggins, of Mrs Broadley and Mrs Mudkin. Was everyone walking around with old or current wounds?

'One day,' Pilpenny continued, 'Finn tells Margaret that he had been digging in the fairy ring. Oh, that upset your mother, Lizzie, didn't it now, because everyone knows you do not mess about with a fairy ring.'

Lizzie turned to me. 'I *told* you, Naomi.'

'But worse yet, Finn tells her he dug up a sack of gold, and she got so mad at him, she hit him with a flour sack and the flour went all over the place so's they both looked like ghosts, and she told him to put that gold back in the fairy ring, and don't you know, it was the next day he died.' Again, she pressed her hand to her chest.

'Did he put the gold back?'

'I don't think there was any gold in the first place, but even if there was and even if he did put it back, it was too late, wasn't it?'

Lizzie said, 'That is entirely too creepy, and I wish you'd not told us that.'

We found the trunk, and with the help of the key and a screwdriver, it opened. A burst of lavender rose out of the trunk, so strong you'd have thought someone had just picked a fresh bunch of it and tossed it inside. Near the top were an old coat and scarf and a faded quilt.

'Nothing very remarkable here,' Lizzie said.

I pulled out a pair of leather boots, scuffed and worn; a pair of woollen gloves; and a heavy woollen shirt. There were a few more articles of clothing and a tin box containing a mirror, a comb, two keys, a few loose buttons and what looked like an identity card of some sort, creased as if it might have been carried in a pocket or wallet. At the bottom of the box was a small latch.

I fiddled with the latch until it came loose, revealing another compartment in the bottom of the box. In that compartment was a sack, and when I lifted it, it jingled as if it held coins.

'Uh-oh,' I said, dropping the sack on the floor.

CHAPTER 54

Across the Ocean: The Mail

I t was a sunny, calm day in Blackbird Tree as the mailman made his rounds.

Down at the church, Mrs Mudkin examined the cheque in her hand and then reread the attached note: *From an anonymous donor. Please use these funds to help the unfortunate souls.* She looked again at the cheque, holding it up to the light. 'Is this *real*?'

Up the road a ways, Mrs Cupwright opened an envelope and called to her husband. 'Come here and look at what came in the mail.'

Mr Cupwright was lying on the sofa, the newspaper over his face. 'None of my business,' he said.

Mrs Cupwright smiled. 'Okey doke, then.' She slipped the cheque into her purse.

Crazy Cora was sitting on her porch with her grown son, watching the workers repair her damaged roof, when the mailman handed her an envelope.

'Well, lookee here, a letter from Dora. She's coming to visit.'

'All the way from Ireland?'

'Yep. Guess I'd better wash the windows.'

Mr Thomas Canner held an envelope in his hand, turning it over and over, and holding it up to the window. He returned to his favourite chair and read the letter from his brother. Once. Twice. Three times. He slipped the letter inside *Tales of Ireland* and pressed the book to his chest.

I'm going to Ireland, he thought. *At last I am going to Ireland.*

Later that day, two boys stood amid the remains of Joe and Nula's barn. The taller boy, Bo, scuffed ashes with his boot. 'Might find some stuff in here.'

'It's pretty much picked over,' the other boy said.

Near where they stood, a ring of mushrooms had sprouted overnight.

'I still don't get it. Somebody's *giving* us the property? Why would they do that? And what about that girl Naomi and the old lady? What will happen to them?'

'They'll be OK.'

'What makes you so sure?'

'Just a feeling, that's all.'

CHAPTER 55

Mary-Mary and the Gold

In the sack that we'd found in Finnbarr's trunk were six golden coins.

'*Ach*,' said Pilpenny, backing away. 'The fairy gold?'

'Don't touch it!' Lizzie said.

In the next morning's mail – or 'post,' as Pilpenny called it – came an envelope addressed to me, and inside was a piece of blue paper. On it, in a child's printing, was a poem – or a story – or something in between:

> *Sometimes I think the cloud in the sky is a baby*
> *waiting for life*
> *At dawn, I climb to my rooftop and watch*

the baby unfold
Sometimes I think the cloud in the sky is a bird in a nest
At dawn, I climb to my rooftop and watch the bird fly
Sometimes I think the cloud in the sky is a story
waiting to be read
At dawn, I climb to my rooftop and read that story
The story about me, the cloud, and the rooftop.

—Naomi Deane, age 8

On the back, written in pencil:

Dear Mr Farley,
I am sorry about your arm. I know how it feels. I
hope you like the poem.

And then I remembered when I had written it. It was when I'd seen Mr Farley outside the boarding house one day shortly after he'd returned to Blackbird Tree. Bo and another boy were standing on the corner, pointing at him and laughing. It made me mad. I went home and wrote him that poem. I had forgotten this completely and wondered why he had sent it back to me now and how he knew where to send it.

At the very bottom of the page, in faint pencil, was this new note:

I like your poem.
Your friend,
Artie Farley

Also in the envelope was a square of paper with these words on it, in elegant script:

> *Naomi,*
> *Your mother was an aide at the hospital when Artie*
> *met her. She was kind to him when few other people*
> *were.*
> *Fondly,*
> *Hazel Wiggins*

Did a delicate cobweb link us all, silky lines trailing through the air?

CHAPTER 56

Across the Ocean: True as True

In Blackbird Tree, at Tebop's General Store, the talk was about mysterious letters.

'And I heard that Mrs Mudkin—'

'And what about Crazy Cora and—'

'I saw a florist truck from up in Ravensworth over at Witch Wiggins's house—'

'No!'

'True as true can be. My sister's brother-in-law works up there and he said a big fat bunch of roses was ordered up for Witch Wiggins—'

'From who?'

'From that Dingle Dangle fellow, that's what I hear.'

'No!'

'True as true can be.'

CHAPTER 57

Standing on the Moon

Mr Dingle took one of the gold pieces to have it appraised. 'Don't want to arouse suspicion – or greed – by taking all six pieces,' he said. 'I'll say it belongs to a rich client in London.'

Before he left, he added, 'Meanwhile, Naomi, you need to be thinking about the dogs.'

The dogs.

My fear of dogs had become too big, like a massive expanding clod, making me feel heavy, filled with clay. Sybil's dogs had been staying with Mr Dingle's family, awaiting their intended return to Rooks Orchard. Lizzie said, 'Naomi, here is my idea. Will you listen for one minute? We will bring in one of the dogs – on a leash – and you will just stand there, maybe let her smell you. We'll bring Sadie – Auntie Pilpenny says she's completely gentle. Then tomorrow, maybe two minutes. Then three minutes and on like that until you feel comfortable, OK, will you do it, will you, please?'

On the first day, the minute was agony. I cried.

On the second day, the two minutes were agony. I cried.

On the third day, the three minutes were agony. I threw up.

Later that day, Lizzie and I found clay in the stream that ran beneath the Crooked Bridge. We made clay dogs and perched them on the bridge railing to dry. I still carried a lump of wet clay when we visited Sybil's grave and then Finnbarr's stone beneath the oak tree.

'Poor Finnbarr boy,' Lizzie said. 'Naomi, think of it. If Finnbarr had grown up, maybe my mother would have married him and never have moved to America or saved your life.'

I knelt beside Finnbarr's stone. 'Lizzie, we don't know that she saved my life.'

'Well, *I* know it,' Lizzie said, 'and if she hadn't saved your life, you might be dead.'

'You crawdad.'

But I thought about all the things that had to have spun into place in order for us to be alive and for us to be right there, right then. I thought about the few things we thought we knew and the billions of things we couldn't know, all spinning, whirling out there somewhere.

In the middle of the next week, I went to the moon. I saw the brilliantly blue earth, swaddled in swirls of white. I saw what it was and what it would be. I saw its smallness and its largeness.

That day, I looked into the eyes of a white and tawny foxhound named Sadie and fell in love.

Soon Sadie was joined by Maddie. Those eyes, those faces, their gentle manner, their silky coats: they bewitched me.

Outside with me and Lizzie, they ran and rolled and licked and nuzzled. They bounded back to us and leaned against our legs.

I understood what I had missed.

When Mr Dingle returned with the gold piece, he said, 'The appraiser was fearful. He said that, yes, it appears to be real gold but he did not want to touch it or have it in his shop because of this mark.' With a pen, Mr Dingle tapped an indentation in the centre of the coin. It resembled a half-moon. 'That, apparently, is the mark of fairy gold.'

'I *knew* it,' Lizzie said.

I wished we could stuff the gold coins back in the donkey's ears – and said so – but then I had to explain Joe's story about the donkey's ears.

Mr Dingle said, 'I suppose you could do that, stuff it back in the donkey's ears.'

'What?' Lizzie said. '*What?*'

'Lizzie, you do know we don't really mean to put it in a donkey's ears?'

'Oh. I knew that.' You could see her rearranging a few things in her head. 'Then let's rebury it in the fairy ring. It's only right.'

And so we did, or rather I did, because Lizzie refused to touch the ground inside the ring.

Lizzie felt obliged to offer an apology to the fairies. 'We are sorry,' she said, 'that Finnbarr stole it in the first place. We didn't mean to touch it.'

And so we spent our days roaming the orchards with the dogs and wading the stream and digging for clay and wandering through the vast house. Nula missed Joe, but she was content at Rooks Orchard, and although Pilpenny mourned Sybil, she was cheered by rediscovering her niece, Lizzie.

Lizzie was nearly delirious in her joy. 'We have a home!' she exclaimed each morning. 'Plum jam!' She flew down the hallways and up the stairs. 'We're just like sisters, Naomi, you and me – but we won't be the kind who get mad at each other or fight over a boy and never see each other again, will we? We won't do *that*.'

And me? One night early on, I dreamed that I was trying to get back to Blackbird Tree. I was following a rook and lost my way on a crooked bridge and landed in a hay loft and someone was calling, 'Mary, Mary.' And then, 'Naomi, Naomi.' I told the voice, 'Naomi can't stay; she's on the ladder,' and I flew back to Ireland on the back of the rook.

When I woke, I felt such freedom, such lightness. Lizzie and I had a roof over our heads, we had food, we had Nula and

Pilpenny, we had ladders and dogs, a creek and clay, and we had each other – with all the good and bad that might come with that.

But not *too* much bad, I hoped.

One day, about a month after we'd arrived, I was up in the oak tree near the fairy ring and Lizzie was in a nearby tree pulling plums. The dogs were trolling along beneath the trees, sniffing at fallen fruit. Rook was flying above.

'Lar-de-dar,' Lizzie was singing. 'Oh, lar-de-dar-dar!'

I saw him first. He was coming towards me, sunlight on his hair, freckles on his cheeks.

'Hey, tree girl,' he called.

'Oh, lar-de-dar,' Lizzie sang. *'Lar-de-dar-dar.'*

Sharon Creech

is the internationally renowned author of the Carnegie Medal winner, *Ruby Holler*, and was shortlisted for the Costa Award for *Chasing Redbird*. In the US *Walk Two Moons* won the Newbery Medal and *The Wanderer* was a Newbery Honor Book. She has two grown-up children and lives with her husband in upstate New York.

Her books have sold over a million copies worldwide.

The Unfinished Angel

SHARON CREECH

'Peoples are strange!
The things they are doing and saying — sometimes they make
no sense. Did their brains fall out of their heads?'

Angel is having an identity crisis when he meets Zola –
a talkative young girl who moves into Angel's tower
high in the Swiss Alps. 'This Zola is a lot bossy,' Angel
thinks. But out of their bickering an unexpected
friendship forms, and their teamwork is about to benefit
the entire village ...

This endearingly funny and life-affirming novel by
Carnegie Award-winning author,
Sharon Creech, reminds us that
magic can be found in even the
most ordinary acts of kindness, and
that it's the little things that make
life great.

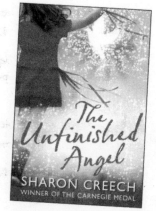

9781849390835 £5.99

The Unfinished Angel

'Sharon Creech tells wonderful, mesmerising stories that draw you in and wrap themselves around you with characters that grow as the story unravels.'
Daily Telegraph

'Comical and moving novel . . .
full of accidental wisdom about the inhumanity of humans.'
The Sunday Times

'Inventive, sassy and gutsy . . . an endlessly witty and life-affirming read.'
Booksellers' Choice, The Bookseller

'A magical story that's truly original, touching and funny.'
Julia Eccleshare

'Some books are absolute magic, and this is one of them.'
School Library Journal

'(An) endearing contemporary fable . . . moving, funny and sweet . . .
and begging to be read aloud.'
Kirkus, Starred Review

'Unbelievably sweet little novel.'
Wall Street Journal

'The moment I finished *The Unfinished Angel*, I began to read it again.
I suspect you will, as well.'
Write Away

'Deceptively simple, full of wit, humour and insight.'
Booktrust, Best Book Guide

'Sharon's ability to have fun with language is evident throughout her books.'
Carousel

A Lovereading4kids' Best Children's Book of 2010

The Boy
on the Porch

SHARON CREECH

When John and Marta found the boy on the
porch, they were curious, naturally, as to why he
was there – and they hadn't expected him to stay,
not at first, but he did stay, day after day, until it
seemed as if he belonged.

As the couple's connection to the mysterious boy
grows, the three of them blossom into an unlikely
family. But where has he come from and to whom
does he belong?

In this moving story, Carnegie
Medal winner Sharon Creech
poignantly reminds us of the
surprising relationships that
can bloom when generosity
and unconditional love prevail.

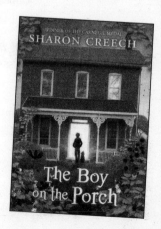

9781849397728   £9.99